LUSIS LOST

LUSIS LOST

Nicholas E. Bertram

PALMETTO
P U B L I S H I N G
Charleston, SC
www.PalmettoPublishing.com

Copyright © 2024 by Nicholas E. Bertram

All rights reserved

No portion of this book may be reproduced, stored in a retrieval system, or transmitted in any form by any means–electronic, mechanical, photocopy, recording, or other–except for brief quotations in printed reviews, without prior permission of the author.

Paperback ISBN: 979-8-8229-4411-4
eBook ISBN: 979-8-8229-4412-1

TABLE OF CONTENTS

Prologue 1
1 3
2 8
3 11
4 15
5 19
6 29
7 32
8 38
9 43
10 56
11 67
12 71
13 76
14 80
15 83
16 89

PROLOGUE

A boy was lost in a dense, foggy forest. He had just finished driving through the night from California in complete isolation. No radio, no company, just alone with his thoughts and the vibrant vistas of the great American West. After finishing his first year at university, he began feeling profoundly detached from the journey he was sent out to pursue. Once busy coping with what the world had become, he now pulled over to the side of the road to what appeared to be the remains of a long-forsaken trail and began to run downhill. Running down trails had always brought him peace, as he enjoyed its self-regulated danger. Each step was a form of falling, an improvisation, a graceful flail. However, this trail was different, and he knew it as he tied his withered laces. The dirt was loose, and the trees breathed as if recognizing his tension. Its narrow lanes, canopied by ancient spruce and bristlecone trees, marked an environment long ignored by any human being. This is what he was after—true solitude.

Though he always consulted nature and physical exertion as introspective and therapeutic tools, he recently grew bitter toward what he called "the national park experience." He described it as an ingenuine representation of nature, just a collection of preserved vistas devoid of the actual energy that exists in the wilderness. It was as if every bird, bear, and insect knew they were experiencing a sort of glorified captivity. This concept of glorified captivity haunted this boy, as he genuinely felt that something unknown and tyrannical lurked behind his and everyone else's existence. Something superior yet unexplored was successfully spellbinding the collective human experience. It didn't matter whether it was intentional or not; its existence was enough. He discovered that the value systems that he was once subscribed to were not of his conception but the conception of a sick society that no longer recognized the sacred. This drove him to hate the things he had embraced to individualize himself, the silly things he would do to portray himself as somehow unique or superior to other people. But he grew frustrated as he watched everyone choose to preserve their idiosyncrasies rather than learn from the best among them. Especially the best who have ever been among us.

But this boy's intentions for this run were distant even to him, and especially to the ones he loved. Still, he left with nothing but the worn shoes on his feet and the shorts from a forgotten friend around his waist. Now throwing himself through the forest sprinkled with Indian paintbrush he is free to reconstruct his psychological landscape to perform with him harmoniously. No longer against him. This boy chose to carry this tension into the world he was growing to fear in an attempt to become its symbolic antidote. It was clear to him that there was no higher goal—to work and sacrifice toward releasing the spiritual tension carried by all the men and women he had ever encountered. To do it, he had to offer something definitively new. He didn't want to find a new shade or hue; he sought the fourth primary color that couldn't help but blend into the reality we all share.

1

I'm currently at dinner with my best friend, who, to my luck, also happens to be the girl I love. We are a team and a new standard of companionship that our peers long to achieve for themselves. We have just finished our first year at university, and we love each other as unconditionally as our maturity allows. I decided to stay with her and her family for the time being. They are wholesome, happy people from a much different culture than mine. Connections with people like this, in a way, transcend the time shared together. It doesn't matter how long we are together or apart; the interaction remains natural and healing, the kind of thing you can depend on forever. Her parents are beautiful, well-intentioned people. Both have immigrated from their respective countries to the United States and have achieved notable material success. They like me, but they see through me, and not necessarily in a negative way. They just have the life experience to understand who and what I am.

My perpetual restlessness, anxious articulations, and competitive spirit expose my unfortunate precondition. Though we deeply care for one another, the underpinning story for how we will live our lives was too different. To no fault of our own, our parents provided us both with contradicting philosophies for how one should approach life. They lived deep within us; even if we preferred to compromise, we would have only neutered one another. Those differences lay so deep that discovering them was both paradoxically obvious and abstruse. Fundamentally, I was beginning to understand that what I needed from my life would have kept her from what she needed. Yet, it is almost guaranteed that surrendering my needs for hers would lead my life to a safer and potentially happier place. Her parents are spectacularly conscious of this in a nonverbal type of way, and they are beginning to doubt my ability to let go of the almost delusional ambitions I have in store. But they are right. I refuse to stop feeding this part of myself. Instead, I continue to strengthen and sharpen it. I am realizing that fundamentally, it won, and now my delightful codependency with her can no longer continue.

I've been sitting there at their dinner table thinking and am just now noticing the unfortunate length of my silence. The antique chair I am sitting in requires far too much concentration to avoid making any cracking or snapping sounds. The softness of the lighting is obstructed by the city lights coming from the smoggy million-dollar view that neither satisfied nor impressed. To no surprise, her mother catches on and says, "Julius! What do you think?"

Without knowing what she was referring to, I quickly respond in a humorous tone, "You know, I think it's probably a chicken-and-egg issue!" while grabbing my partner's hands with an unapologetic smile. I excuse myself and head for the bathroom.

My stomach is churning. I'm often disturbed by my capacity to pretend. I am truly a natural actor. I have a greater tendency to chameleon my way through situations rather than being who I truly am. But I have written off that inquiry into who I am as a fairly trivial introspection. I had grown content with simply being who I needed to be in any environment I found myself in. Optimizing only for what I deemed to be effective, I demonstrated a personality that possessed an off-the-cuff grandiosity and eccentricity but no real utility.

As I come back out, they begin to clear the table. She warmly smiles at me, and I begin to help. I quickly occupy the role of tonight's dishwasher so I can continue reasoning to myself with as little interruption as possible.

Reasoning about what exactly?

Well, a decision, a decision regarding whether or not I should do what I fantasize about or stay here and continue to postpone the life my altered self seeks to create. Or am I simply telling myself a story to reappropriate my purpose, to develop the habits of those I admire? But my mind has already been made up. The only thing to do now is to determine how I'll leave.

I finish the final dish and sit down on the couch with her father. We share a glass of wine and enjoy the silence. It was a wine that he had made himself a few years prior, and like everything this family set their mind to, it was wonderful. He and I were close. We loved to tell each other stories and even had playful political debates where we almost always disagreed. He was better than most men, certainly better than me. He was the sort of person who knew what was right and wrong. But not from some moral framework forced upon him. His was developed through dense experience. He was authentic and lived in a way where any one film wouldn't do his life justice. Life for him was a journey of recreating oneself again and again, grounded in the curiosity of his inner child. He was an engineer of experience, an alchemist of playful and lasting moments. Everyone who touched his life, no matter how brief or infrequent, truly loved him.

The mother sits with us and makes sly remarks, thanking me for doing the dishes. I smile and nod and begin to feel my anxiety grow again. I was generally more anxious around her mother as she was the sort of person who did not believe in the existence of psychic abilities. However, if anyone had them, it was undoubtedly her. I was raised among provocative and confronting patriarchs, so I rarely came in contact with anyone who would summon feelings of inadequacy in me like she would. But, again, this was a quality of hers I admired. She was wiser than she gave herself credit. She always tried to communicate that people must focus on what didn't come naturally to them. She loved speaking philosophically about how difficult it was for her to not instinctually parent the way her mother parented her. Despite deeply understanding her mother's flaws as a parent, she felt trapped and destined to repeat it, almost acknowledging that she already had. There was a pang of visible guilt to her every time it came up. She knew that if you were not highly skilled in your ability to concentrate, then your freedoms were much more limited than they appeared. For her, it was a tragedy that she had discovered this fact so late in life.

I dial back into the conversation while Ellen DeGeneres rants at some unamused celebrity in the background. I gesture to Cathryn that I'm ready to be alone, and she sets up our escape.

She stands and yawns. "Well, Mom and Dad, thank you so much for dinner. It was really great. As you know, Julius and I are very tired from our drive from Santa Barbara today and are just about ready for bed."

I make the appropriate and polite remarks back, and we head upstairs. As we enter Cathryn's bedroom, a rush of relief washes over me as I see my belongings all together and organized. I sit on the end of the bed and calmly embrace her, squeezing the purity I cherished so much. I say good night to her and head downstairs into the guest room, where I generally work on various things before going to bed. It's a clear night. She looks at me as if acknowledging my internal conflict by briefly hugging me from behind. I grab my only bag containing my bare essentials, get in my car, and drive away.

2

As I run down this trail, knowing I must eventually ascend that which I am plummeting into, my frustration at myself continues. I can't escape it. I can no longer tell if I'm supposed to continue the seemingly circular investigation in my mind or if I should just let go. Letting go has always been portrayed as a more straightforward matter than I have experienced it to be. Even still, I developed the mantra, "Let go and grow," something I repeat to myself over and over again until I am convinced of its truth. I typically run to music to distract myself from these unresolved threads of thought that no longer bring me philosophical insight. However, I need space from that deep, dark mirror. My phone simply represents the extremes of my new nature. It facilitates the learning, reading, and listening that expands my mind into new realms of supposedly productive contemplation. However, it also encourages my tendencies for interpersonal cruelty and perversion. Like the rest of my peers, I am ill-prepared for this sort of technological empowerment. So I leave it in an abandoned car with my once-valuable possessions.

My actions of late are different from how I once conducted myself. Much of my fear comes from how my friends and family perceive me. I see how some of my actions can be seen as nihilistic or selfish, and this hurts me, as I intensely dislike these characterizations and the people I know that way. Yes, I am distant from them. But it is for them. I have to create the space to uncover what it is I'm chasing. I don't know what stories created my North Star and if it is a place worth heading toward. But who in our culture can trust the amalgamation of programming and influence we are all thrown into? So much of what we consume is emotional pornography. Our relationship with our feelings has been tampered with, seeded with expectations of what our own experience with them will be, moonshot into a domain that is simply unreachable. Our media takes our feelings of aspiration, anger, and love and harmfully exaggerates our experience of them.

The only courage we are allowed to express is simulated, and now we can only relate to the fallen. We no longer celebrate our ascended masters because we no longer have any. We embrace this new way of life because our individual lives are far less extreme than those before us. We are deceived into believing that this is the best it's ever been, epically free to escape into obscure addictions that free us from the mundanity of modern life, addictions that ordinarily manifest in the form of something that one materially or chemically consumes. Yet, it also comes to form in the retelling of fictitious stories about ourselves or the honoring of artists and celebrities who vicariously provide you with the experiences you thought the world promised. But after all, none of us are taught how to concentrate. We aren't taught how to use our emotions to motivate or free us from faithlessness. Whether it be the faith in yourself or a higher power, we lack the ability to cultivate, visualize, and fight for our collective potential. We are assumed to depend on institutions of power that no longer value us. We are asked, "What is your dream job? Who is your ideal master?" rather than, "What do you want to accomplish? What do you want to explore?" We are taught to work alone and for ourselves. We are given a flawed value system that blinds us to anything higher than ourselves, let alone the highest thing to aim toward...

This is what my body does to me. It forces my mind to synthesize itself through exertion. It only allows me to experience temporary peace through conceptualizing ideas like these. I feel for those who have not yet uncovered this truth for themselves. I am not unique, and the primary dimension of myself that differentiates most is a commitment to exertion. I am not content subscribing to a life riddled with feelings of inadequacy, anxiety, and melancholy. I refuse the seemingly inevitable dependency on the looking-forward-tos and permission-seeking. I require a path with consequences—one where the truest, best parts of myself are forced through, not performed.

3

I am now even further down, at least seven miles, and am beginning to feel fatigued. I stop for a moment and patiently absorb the thrill of true isolation. The moonlit night, the fog across the canopy, and the mountainous landscape lighten and rapture my spirit. As my breath returns to me, an emerald moth appears, soaring past my left ear. As if to gain my attention, it circles me once, twice, and ultimately soars down the path I had questioned giving up on. So, I continue, embracing the moth as a temporary guide, pushing me to ignore my constructed limits.

As the sun starts to set, the trail begins to level out. Fear rushes over me as I realize my chances of getting to my car and drinking water have already passed. So, I continue, passing tree after tree under the moon's luminous eye. "I have passed a wall, which many runners more skilled than I speak of, and am now in my strongest stride yet, the tension in my hands is gone, the breaths through my nose are thorough, and I am free from my petty reflections. Unlike many troubles in my life that I am seemingly victim to, I have created this one solely on my own. This morbid comfort feels me up and down, aligning myself with *true* nature, a nature that

I always seem to seek, a sort of electrical stillness that only exists in the wild.

I am beginning to lose my thirst, my fatigue, my self-doubt. Even time begins to distort. In moments such as these, when I feel I have achieved true oneness with my environment, time dissipates, and I wrangle with new thought forms involving matters superior to any individual's life, models of existence that I can hardly process into any visual or linguistic domain. It is freedom in its most productive mode, where one unintentionally investigates what lies between metaphors and connotations. I continue this psychophysical dance until realizing I had lost the original trail. I notice the chirrs from my feet, crushing the dried pine needles beneath me. Nevertheless, I carry forward, zigzagging between the trees as if I were both chasing and being chased.

I begin to hope for a clearing to appear, and fear again reintroduces itself. My right foot slips on a damp, loose pile of needles. To catch myself, I quickly shoot my left leg forward. But instead, it is caught in a large root, and I fall to my chest. My foot has just been forced into a disastrous spot, and a rush of pain begins to flow through me. My Achilles tendon appears to be distinctly torn, at least partially, and I can no longer put pressure on it. I do my best to ignore the layman's truth and begin to crawl with my weight toward my right side. In a one-legged bear crawl, I methodically make my way to what I hope is an elevated clearing. Time has again taken on its familiar form, and it has become difficult to judge my progress. The dense canopy of the forest thoroughly blocks the moonlight. I hear rustling and grow paranoid that something may have begun to stalk me.

Nevertheless, I continue, dragging myself deeper into the unknown. The emerald moth appears again, somehow soaring with a more excellent luminescence. I begin to hear a deep, hypnotizing tone. It kicks me from the negative space my mind has fallen into and lifts me slowly into an ecstatic vibration. My vision begins to distort, and my breaths become brief and shallow. Suddenly, I hear a whistle behind me. I turn around and see nothing. I hear the whistle again, but to my left, I faintly witness a pair of antlers pass behind a tree. I call out, "Hello! Who's there? I need help."

I stop and fall to my knees. The forest darkens and becomes eerily quiet. I can barely see, and I call again, "Hello, is anyone there?"

Six figures reveal themselves, surrounding me. At the sides are four tall, slender men covered in dark-red hooded robes. Their curved horns tear through their hoods and are drenched in black oil. Their stench is horrid. They quickly grabbed my hands as they approach me, sniffing and licking them. Their skin is burned and wrinkled. Their fingernails are long and infected, with tongues that are dry and coarse. As they touch me, I feel my mind fog and disassociate, my body nauseating. I reach to get away, and I cannot move. The two others in front of me are barely in sight. They continue to walk toward me with an unnatural, almost paranormal pace. One is a beautiful brunette woman with hair down to her waist. She is utterly nude, aside from a large mask that covers her entire face and neck. The mask has large black owl-like eyes that consume all the light around us. Holding her hand is a hairless, androgynous man in all black. He continues to whistle as they approach me. As he gets close, the four in red scurry away fearfully, disappearing out of sight. The two now stand in front of me.

The man walks behind me, gently taking hold of my long hair from behind. The woman continues her approach. I get increasingly nauseous as the deep, hypnotizing tones become louder and louder. The man yanks my hair back, revealing the strange purple and black storm circling above us. He then rips off the woman's mask, revealing her eyes to be the same as those on the mask. As her face approaches mine, I can see the entire night sky in her eyes—mesmerizing, glistening stars and planets. The man places each of his hands on the back of our necks, gently guiding her face toward mine until she begins to kiss me. I feel as though I am beginning to float upward until I realize I have lost my ability to move.

Suddenly, a light floods the space, and a small device detonates, releasing a vast cloud of smoke, causing myself and the others to cough and gag. The heavy scent of smoke lingers in my nostrils, making it hard to breathe. The forest around me is engulfed in chaos. Flames dance wildly, devouring everything in their path. Panic surges through my veins as I try to understand what's happening. Through the smoke, I catch sight of a figure stumbling toward me. It's a woman, disheveled and coughing violently.

"You," she gasps, crouching beside me. "Come with me. We have to get out of here." I nod, unable to form words as I take in the destruction surrounding us. Together, we stumble through the smoke and flames and make our escape.

4

"My name is Bona. It is nice to meet you."

"Nice to meet you, Bona. Who were those people? What was that?"

"Some people call them stalkers. Others call them inverters. They have always existed in these woods but never this comfortably. Their numbers have grown so much over the past few years."

"What were they doing to me?"

"Cheap tricks, nothing to worry about. You would have been in a lot of trouble if you were eight or nine years younger. It's honestly highly unusual for them to prey on someone as old as you."

"Oh, I see."

"Yeah, you aren't what they typically look for, if you catch my drift. They used to only have a couple of camps around the country, but now they seem to be everywhere, more resourceful and more intelligent. I'm really concerned about where this country and this world is heading. We have always been deceived but deceived in the name of our protection. Now, they are taking advantage of us. The most vulnerable among us. Which means everything has to be reset."

"Reset to what? What do you mean?"

"We need to start fresh. Start again. But we can only do that on the other side of some major discovery. Otherwise, people will continue not knowing the difference between up and down."

Bona and I finally approach the front door of a cabin. We climb up the twelve stone steps, symbolizing the end of my journey. I set myself to the right-hand side of the door. Bona goes inside, and I begin to reflect on whatever lessons I had learned from whatever just happened, which seem inconsequential as the pain from my left foot begins to mount. She returns and hands me a large Mason jar full of water. Squatting in front of me, she grabs and examines my injured foot. "This will take time to heal, and you'll stand no chance of hiking or riding out of here from wherever you came from for some time…So! Unless you have someone nearby who can come get you, you'll have to stay here with me until you're better."

She was a beautiful and imposing woman with exceptional energy and body language. Her skin was this remarkable honey color I had only seen a handful of times before. Her hair was dark and spun into a youthful French braid that reminded me of how my sister used to do hers. I instantly knew she was my clear superior, and I had much to learn from her. Abruptly, she whistles at me to come inside. The cabin is large, with tall ceilings highlighted by hand-carved beams. There are only a few rooms, as one primary living space dominates most of the square footage. The main room is centered around a massive window I had seen from outside. At the base of the window sits a large desk covered with books, loose yellow paper, and a sizable military-grade laptop.

She points me toward a leather couch to the left side of the room as she prepares a bucket of ice water. While making her way to the sofa, I noticed my need for an explanation of who she was and how she had gotten here. But she withdraws and places the bucket and towel by my leg. To my surprise, I have miraculously run into a person who is not impressed, concerned, or interested in how and why I got here. I am treated like an ill animal rather than a boy who needs discipline or compassion. Strangely, this comforts me, as I have grown unfortunately accustomed to ineffective and earnestly kind people.

Sat on her couch with my foot in the ice bucket, I take a deep breath and communicate my gratitude. She walks toward me, pleased that I've made myself comfortable.

"So, what's your name, sweetheart?" she chirps while extending her hand.

I stutter as I receive her warmth. "Oh, I'm Julius. Thank you for all this and for allowing me into your home. It's quite something."

"Thank you. It's made entirely from the lumber on this land and is totally self-sufficient. It was once a place of great purpose. But listen, I've never been one for dilly-dallying, and I'm certainly not going to start now by virtue of a peculiar visitor. Let me show you where you'll be staying."

I stand and follow her down the hall in a pathetic limp. It's longer than I had expected it to be. It's lined by ancient artwork containing unique symbols I was not familiar with. Punctuated at the end of the hallway is a tall gothic mirror that is smokey and difficult to look into. She opens the door to the room I'd be staying in—a pile of papers, one pair of pants, and a white T-shirt are on the bed. The clothing is wrinkled and was thrown onto the bed casually. I have a feeling they are the remains of an old boyfriend. She points to the papers, saying, "I've left you this. You should take a shower and read it afterward. I want to hear your thoughts on it. Not like you have anything else to do."

With a smirk, she leaves the room, closing the door behind her as I head to the shower. I sit on the smoothed slate tiles and breathe purposefully under searing hot water. As my mind grows quiet, I quickly appreciate the energy of Bona's isolated Wyoming home. My mind has taken a liking to the place. I haven't experienced this quality of inner peace since childhood when I'd frequently wander along Oregon's southern coastline alone. I do this for a while until finishing the shower with the water on its coldest setting. I turn it off, go to bed, and fall asleep.

5

I change into the clothes that Bona had given me, grab the pile of papers, and make my way into the living space. On the kitchen counter were two peanut butter and jellies stacked with a tall pulpy drink. I scoff down the two sandwiches and sip on the drink. As she enters the room, she notices my sour face. "Oh, don't be a baby! You should learn to love that stuff!"

"Ok, well. What is it?"

"Broccoli sprouts, Celtic salt, distilled water, and a little bit of pomegranate juice. The broccoli sprouts contain sulforaphane, a chemical that oxidizes the cells in your body that reproduce too quickly. But that doesn't matter. Now! After you finish that, you'll need to ice your foot again and begin reading what I gave you. The bucket is where you left it, and the ice machine is to the left of the dishwasher. I'm going to be on the porch. Call me if you need anything."

I finish the drink, prep my ice bucket, and head toward the couch. Grabbing the papers, I notice their fragile quality and that the words slightly rise off the page like braille. I lay back and begin to read the unnumbered pages:

Qoros is an ancient word used as a title of honor and nobility. It was the Qoros, more than anyone else, who were courageous and destined for glory. They were men of any age who still saw life as a challenge, who faced life with the whole of their vigor, with the whole of their passion. The word indicates the quality of a man, not how old or burdened he had become. They are beings that stand between the world of man and the world of the divine, beings that have access to both, loved and recognized by both. It is only through the embodiment of the Qoros that a man can possibly succeed at the great ordeal of making a journey into the beyond.

The Qoros have a great deal in common with the world of the divine. In their own way, they're both timeless, untouched by age. They are our lost explorers who were once embraced and encouraged to access the world of the Gods for themselves and others. We need them because of their sensitivity and ability to distance themselves from repeating conventional human thoughts and behaviors. They do not interfere unconsciously or consciously with what they have heard or received. For the Qoros, it is about becoming open to the timeless, open to the tranquility and stillness of the Gods. This is the only real maturity there is: the maturity of struggling and exerting oneself beyond the physical world and discovering that your home is somewhere else, unsevered from the world of the fallen—a space of clear conscience, a space in union with your creator.

For modern man experiences only the instant yet insists on sustaining a persona that is ostensibly accustomed to the unknown. For the instants that they indulge are moments overwhelmed with external stimuli, which, by their nature, restrain the necessary introspection for becoming an individual of meaningful utility. The personas of the unchallenged quickly become transparent in the face of internal or external conflict, making these men and women susceptible to enslaving habits. This obsession with stimulation has directed technological innovation away from elevating man's potential, which instead operates mankind and its culture to regress into primordial states where the indulgence of individual desires is prioritized over our civilization's collective potential. For these modern men and women are no longer as human as they may appear. They are convinced they must be, pretend to themselves and to others that they are. Yet they are simply caterpillars bragging about their wings, seeds bragging about their branches. Our children are fresh and smooth, the old are shriveled and stale. The spiritual, the artistic, and the clever all lie somewhere in between. Nearly all never even begin to build their cocoon, as most can't even hear that they aren't what they're meant to be. They forget and ignore just how expensive it is to become human, as the cost is your own being. It is agreeing to be turned inside out until you emerge as an object inside the world within the universe that you are. The price is having to look up at the stars and wonder if there might be life up there—the most absurd of questions considering how you are the light of the stars looking down on yourself.

For modern men only serve mankind as if to know what lies at their end. While none of us really know or understand what ultimately guides us there, these modern men allow men of power to move themselves without knowing that one ultimately moves themself as his soul remains in his own keeping. So, what is one to do when and if he stands before his creator at his end? How will you defend your devotion to man, this world, and their orders? How will you defend your lack of commitment to a higher calling? To the highest calling?

Today, our stories fail to provide modern man with a path toward divinity. Instead, they glorify the lives of lonely antiheroes. A maniacal vein of heroism that leverages the systems of their society to prepare for a journey into the unknown to earn grand material treasures. For in these modern stories following the discovery of such a prize, one discovers that it provides no nourishment. They then choose to forthrightly perpetuate their isolation, ultimately developing self-destructive habits. The heroes of ancient myths, following the discovery of their treasure or prize, would give back to the society that facilitated their development and preparation. However, the antihero at this stage hesitates to give back, as giving back would support in maintaining a reality that failed to bring him bliss or fulfillment. We have been misguided to believe that genuine fulfillment is attainable through an individualized, material world. These stories of the antihero may, however, represent the essential sacrifice of our time, where choosing not to contribute to the paradigm in which we live may have become the more rational conclusion. Yet, these stories of the antihero fail us, as they offer no worthwhile direction following the discovery of what man needs. For what man needs is conquest toward a sacred goal, not a material one. These stories of material pursuits have made the minds of the majority weak, falling comfortable with the logic of victimhood and guidance from false idols.

The masses surrender their will prematurely by camouflaging their being into a framework optimized for general success—lives in service to an anonymous superior. For these Western individuals no longer see themselves as venturous lions but as sheep with uniquely cut coats. Today, perceived identity usurps reality, perceived status usurps divinity, and perceived intelligence usurps strength. This is due to the failure of our mythology in conceptualizing purposeful adventures for modern men during transitionary periods. Therefore, modern men are unconsciously nihilistic spiritually, possessed by logic and redundancy. Our stories fail to carry men toward transcendent action because transcendent action is no longer something we believe in. Our collective belief in the spiritual potential of the human being has never been lower. We carry no ancient traditions; we fight for nothing we can't touch.

Thus, individuals today can only rightly be judged by the collection of their habits and the control of their obscurity, as worthwhile ambitions have become trivialized. Habits are the ultimate judge of man because they function as worthwhile or harmful escapes from the idleness of life. Therefore, assuming disorder and habit as inevitable features of modern life allows one to correctly infer man's value to himself and society. Those who ridicule this logic subscribe knowingly or not to a modern ideology that fundamentally limits the individual, blind to their divine capacity.

Today, this culture permeates as the reigning ideology throughout Western education, film, politics, and media.

To end its pervading rule over the mass's unconscious, the modern individual must be thoroughly dissected and offered a new way to access their inherent divinity. To achieve this, one must dive through the underworld to pass through their own darkness and earn the respect of the wicked forces that prey on them. For darkness in man is omnipresent, something that man wrestles, not controls or buries. Man can only rightly be judged by how his time is exercised in isolation, as it is the only environment they can truly control. Any man who encounters considerable time in proper isolation suspects inevitable introspection. Isolation with the mind is a vital trial for man as it is the only avenue for diagnosing the sources of one's beliefs and motivations.

This method of introspection allows an individual to see what his environment forces him to ignore. It facilitates the creation of a perceptual framework necessary for developing a seemingly new interpretation of his or her place in the world by resolving one's former understanding of self as a delusion not of his or her own creation. But instead, it is the creation of your schooling, family, and culture, influences that are inevitable, essential, and destructive to your evolution. Therefore, uncovering where your psychological tendencies are sourced through a practice of mindful reflection is paramount to improving your well-being and productivity. The current tools of man silence this inner conversation by removing individuals from the inevitability of isolation. Our technological tools are incredible innovations, yet individual consciousness was ill prepared for such a radical empowerment of the mind. Instead, these tools overwhelm and hijack our creative essence, making our minds weaker and more vulnerable to the development of narcissistic delusions that only digest familiar interpretations of truth.

For this reason, what is popular parallels the instant and the despondent. Drugs akin to alcohol remove men from themselves and preserve their ungrounded egotism, though their egos live vicariously through others, not from a place of their own contrivance. A culture that fetishizes ungrounded egotism facilitates an artificial ipseity only valuable to the vain and superficial. This obsession with a one-dimensional self exposes man's unconscious compulsion toward a new metaphysics. Those aware of this need spawn new visions for properly orienting themselves in the world through principles that transcend the virtues of monotheistic desert religions, free from the axial age of great spiritual beings that liberated us from our animalistic nature. Today, these ancient ethics succeed only by containing one's goals and directing them toward blindly serving one God through men of power. But what kind of God would claim to be the only one worthy of worship? What kind of God would guide its adherents through fear and not love? We are contained and encapsulated within a collective mind that simulates the promotion of individuality to improve social and economic metrics void of divine conscience. In function, these ancient scripts promote only the conformity to a passive "kindness," moving no one who requires radical transformation. Monotheistic, creationist stories to such a seeker fail to provide a meaningful superior to surrender to and develop faith in. For these men are left to ascribe themselves to nothing and are all too familiar with isolation.

These men and women, we call the Qoros, beings that link no gratification to stimulation and simulations, beings destined to unlock the divinity within themselves and others.

The Qoros devote their life to exploring sensory limitations. This is found through stillness and silence. For one must create a deep and nurturing relationship with silence. It must be tended to, nurtured, and cared for like a delicate flower. For the Qoros works to become profound daily, with the goal of dissolving the whys, hows, and whats of life. This process of becoming whole through stillness forces man into a constant subconscious state of reflection, thus refining one's ability to perceive the world around them effectively. Through their versatile perception, the Qoros are capable of moving history. They possess spiritual methods and techniques needed to bring people to reality while bringing entire cultures into being. They have sought to solve the problems that man has yet to articulate.

For today, we have an unaccounted-for international elite that fails to lead men toward a spiritual path. They appear morally tolerable from the outside because they do not have to exercise their power openly. The ones we fear are no longer visible. To exercise power publicly would expose that they have the power we fear they have and that they are beginning to lose it. Absolute power is always concealed until it is competently challenged. The Qoros is an entirely separate entity from modern man and this isolated establishment. For the Qoros works to bring upon his suffering before the world could.

Provided that the world guarantees suffering, the Qoros accepts and decides to forthrightly control his own, as suffering is ultimately a state of encountering the unknown. Therefore, the unknown is the Qoros's only frontier.

For it is the source of fear itself, a force that illuminates the antagonist of your soul. Fear is your superior, an antihero of self that spirals you above and below understanding. Seeking to conquer the unknown brings the possibility of divine satisfaction, a state of being that only a Qoros can achieve, a state full of lasting, fulfilling, and permanent truths.

Thus, becoming Qoros is the antidote to the modern man's conflict, a hero's journey that embraces mortality simply to confront it. When authentically embraced, glory will be yours because power has been given to thee. But that power has been taken from others and offered to you. With that power comes duty as you now serve as a bridge between the world of man and the world of the divine. Keep it and hold it as true or you will fall, as you can now become the best of both.

Everything in this Qoros tradition is a part of that one single pattern. We are set free when we see the pattern and give way to the deception. For all that really binds us is our illusory ideas, our concepts. But what is not a concept? What is it to be free?

To see this pattern means not to be taken and raptured in its deception any longer. Nothing could be more crucial.

But it also means the permanent removal of struggle toward your imaginary realities that tether you to the deception, because to try not to be deceived is far more foolish than to be deceived. Talking about the truth signals that you have already lost sight of it. Understand illusion, and you will find the truth right in its center. Create grand philosophical schemes about reality, and you fall straight into deception. Appreciate the power of deception, and you come face-to-face with reality. To run away from deception is to be deceived. But embrace it, and you have reality itself, as the only protection against deception is to surrender to it. By wholeheartedly allowing ourselves to be deceived, we are no longer deceived. And then, we are just like actors. All we have to remember is that real life expects us to act very well—to stay in good conscience, to repent to those who will forgive us mightily.

6

Bona enters the room with a smile as she notices the concentration on my face. I look up and notice she is unusually sweaty.

"So, what do you think?" she said pointedly.

"There's a lot here…I can't say it doesn't resonate. Did you write this? Were you a philosophy professor?"

"Oh no," she responded condescendingly. "I was a professor in behavioral economics at Stanford for a very long fifteen years. I didn't necessarily enjoy my time around other economists. I found they were a bit too arrogant, given how stuck they were in their beliefs. But I grew very comfortable being alone and realized it was a field that required a great deal of multidisciplinary reading. I'm glad that you've connected to it so quickly, though. I know it's dense, but I do believe that people are being taken advantage of to a far greater extent than anyone can consciously appreciate at this moment. But how did you get here, Julius? You haven't asked to call anyone."

In a sarcastic tone, I sighed and asked, "Well, why are you here all by yourself? And how can you possibly afford a place like this working as a professor?" She looked at me up and down and said,

"Julius, I am more than happy to answer any questions you may have for me. However, you are in my home, so the mutually uncomfortable questions will be done on my terms. How did you find yourself lost in Wyoming?"

"Well, I just finished my first year at university in California and I don't really feel it is helping me grow—to, you know, become the person I want to become. I feel as if the parts of myself that make me, me are being refashioned into some kind of bland mediocrity. And my peers, whom I deeply care about, seem completely ok with this. And then when I earn the things people in my social environment long for, it provides me and the higher version of myself with nothing worthwhile. And it doesn't matter how high I climb in these 'social circles,' it simply doesn't work. Yet the most unfortunate part is that I am not alone, and sometimes I feel I am not even a minority. Too often, I feel my feelings in others. I couldn't stand being surrounded by it. It's suffocating, you know? It has this pernicious quality, and my mind was not able to protect itself. So, I ran away. I drove here, to nowhere, to escape. I ran into the woods because the open road was still too familiar. I decided I would seek out anything different from what I was doing to discover a different approach to becoming the person I believe I can be."

"And what is that?"

"Someone free from fear, yet still connected, grounded. I want to earn influence, but not for the sake of it. I want to earn it in the most healthy and meaningful way possible. But the typical paths for achieving this appear ridden with greed and self-sacrifice. And not the righteous sort of sacrifice…no, it's a cyclical compromise of your individuality between you and the ones who care about you. I want to represent an ideal of my own creation, living my life as a type of experiment where my successes and failures can function as lessons that hold universal value. But I fear that this desire is just that…a desire created by a turbulent and unreliable ego."

"I see, but what makes you think that if I were to tell you how to do everything you are asking about, you would then be able to do it? There is a fickle nature to truth, you know? Say you learn something that fails to create that desired or expected change. How true is it, then? For example, how should you or how could you change after learning something as simple as how thoughts and feelings are not tied or tethered to time in the same way our bodies are? What good would that do even if I told you everything you need to know? You don't have the tools or mental models to be able to use the information. Unearned wisdom should be feared. To fall into semiproductive modes of intellectualization, even or especially at a PhD status, should be feared even more."

"I couldn't agree more, and I don't know what to say to that. I never had much say in what I remember. All I can hope to do is continue to work on myself and just see what sticks over time. But I really appreciate all this—this conversation, you allowing me to stay here and sharing these writings. It's really helping."

"Good, Julius. Then you should stay and continue reading. I believe I can help you as long as you help me. We can continue to discuss this tomorrow. I have a lot of work to do."

7

As one of her heels sinks into the grass, Eve, the latest attention-deprived actress, struggles to get her voice heard above the helicopter. "Lionel! I'm going to be late again!"

"Evey! You don't think I know what time it is?" yells Lionel as he finishes stuffing his things into his coral leather bag. Lionel walks out onto his lawn in an expensive, gray-colored suit, a white collared shirt, and orange leather boots. He hustles on board, and they take off.

"I'm going to be late again for my shoot, and you don't care. I'm seriously getting fed up with your shit, Lionel," says Eve with conviction.

"It's just a fucking movie. Please relax. They'll wait for you."

"Just a movie! You're such a prick. You're so stupid, you think anyone can do what I do."

"No, I think anyone who looks like you can do what you do. You know that you found acting amidst your pursuit of fame, not the other way around."

"And what do you do? No one even understands what you do."

"I live the stories that people like you will seek to recreate fifty years from now. You know, after I've let you all understand what I do."

"You don't do shit. All you do is sit on your fucking computer and yell at people."

Ignoring her, Lionel plugs into his phone, parsing through the day's schedule, ignoring the emails flooding his inbox. His father calls him suddenly, and he picks up.

"Hellooo?" Lionel says in a puckish tone.

"What the hell are you up to?! I'm seeing your face all over the television. Everyone has a different story about what you're doing. What's going on?"

"Oh Dad, remember six or seven years ago, I told you I was going to make something that would change the world, and you told me to screw off? Unfortunately, that worked, and I now control more money than you can imagine…Do you want to know what's actually going on, or are you just calling to kick me around?"

"What the hell is going on?"

"Yeah, so do you remember that accounting software Sam and I made? Well, it became popular among these very powerful people, and over the past couple of years, these government agencies around the world have begun using it. The thing is, though, it has basically let my team and me see where and how money flows within all these government institutions. Which, to no one's surprise, is fairly controversial. The US has too many shadow military programs to count, and the French…well the French's corruption is all petty and leisure-based. Great Britain's banks will back anything for a buck, and the Japanese are too smart to continue using us. I just lost them as a client. We actually had to close an entire office out there. But for the most part, business is great. These government bodies are all right. It's disappointing, but you know, you should never expect conspiracy when it can be better explained by stupidity. So, I'm in a unique position to fuck with these people, and I've taken a liking to holding them somewhat accountable for the things they do have control over... which again, is disappointing."

"Jesus Christ, Lionel! How the—!" screams Lionel's father.

"Sorry, Dad, I'm sure this is a lot for you to process, but I can't spend more time on this. Tell Mom I love her." Lionel hangs up the phone as his helicopter lands on 3 World Trade Center.

"How am I going to get to the shoot, Lionel?" Eve says, as if he, too, was concerned about her being late.

"We'll take the car. I have a meeting with one of these Ivy-League assholes anyhow." He looks down at his phone again and sees a message from his driver, William: "Picked up the senator. Ready for you in the garage."

"God, I hate sitting through your meetings. You don't even listen to me. I really don't think this is working out. You're kind of a dick," says Eve in an effort to gain back the attention she never had.

Distracted, Lionel walks straight into the elevator with his head in his phone, nodding. "Yeah baby, whatever you want."

Eve sighs and puts her headphones in.

The car William arrives in is Lionel's favorite. It's a large custom limousine with unusually high-tech gadgets and touch screens all over the car's interior. Despite having one of the most spectacular views of New York City from his office, Lionel enjoys working on the move away from the busyness. As Lionel and Eve enter, the nervous politician awkwardly gawks at Eve as she passes him to get to the other end of the car. He's clearly more used to others waiting on him as opposed to having to wait for some young guy and his girlfriend.

Sarcastically, Lionel greets him, "Hello, Senator. How are you today?"

"Cut the crap, Lionel. Have you seen the latest budget proposals? They want to increase military spending again, and I owe them a favor. I kept putting it off, but now my reelection is coming up, and if I don't vote this through, there is no way I'll get the nomination."

"Relax, Senator, it's too early to talk with so little imagination. Has your guy in the house got his infrastructure money yet?"

"Well, no, but—"

"Ok, that's fine. I can siphon out half a yard from Brazil's agriculture programs. They won't notice, and they'd be using that money to destroy the Amazon anyhow."

"Jesus Christ," the senator says under his breath, sinking into his seat.

"It'll be accessible by the end of the week. If your boy fails to roll out those fucking projects within the next three months, you and I are going to have a problem. Get me those permits."

"Goddammit, you know how incompetent Rosemann is," says the senator, raising his voice.

"As far as I'm concerned, you all are. Now, let's talk about my contracts."

"No disrespect Lionel, but how the fuck am I supposed to go in there and explain that you need another five billion dollars? You got two just six months ago, and we have nothing to show for that. If we do this, we are going to get it up the ass by the media from both sides! Excuse my language, honey," he adds, gesturing to Eve, unsure whether or not she was paying attention. William stops the car, and Eve hops out as if Lionel and the senator weren't there, slamming the door behind her.

"Senator, like last time, this money is all being spent on R & D to ensure this country is safer than the others. And because I work with other countries in the interest of this one, nothing that I just said can be understood publicly. So, in short, if the US Senate and I aren't growing together, we are dying together. The Pentagon still thinks this country must protect itself in military terms. But since the fucking hydrogen bomb came about back in nineteen-fucking-fifty-two, things have changed. I've seen your budgets for these ridiculous fighter jets, but today, all warfare is conducted in cyberspace through financial institutions, and in order to continue to pretend that this country is growing, you need me to protect you."

"This is where you lose me, Lionel. I don't care why; I just need something to tell them."

Lionel pushes a button on the console. "William, don't leave yet." For the first time in the conversation, Lionel looks the senator in the eyes, gets up, and sits beside him.

"Listen, you're just not being honest about the new reality you live in, Senator. All of your feedback loops got mucked up, meaning that now, when an 'institution' accuses you of something, the world gets to offer their opinion before your snobby ass can gracefully respond or rebut. It's not convenient for anyone trying to do anything because it's just another hoop to jump through. Nuanced challenges like this are hard for some people to get their heads around. They are popping up all over the place, all the time, and it doesn't matter what the technological conditions of the time are. Pareto distributions somehow infected our world a long, long time ago."

"What's a Pareto distribution? I don't know what you're talking about. You're just trying to make me feel stupid again."

"Get out, Senator, and don't ask me again how to do your job. Makes you look like a clown." Lionel pinches the senator's nose, making a squeaking sound.

Grunting and rolling his eyes, the senator steps out of the car, visibly frustrated. Lionel rolls down the window. "So, when will I see you next?" says the senator earnestly.

"Honestly, you're too neurotic for me, Senator, so hopefully not any time soon." Handing the senator a card, he says, "You now communicate through one of my new assistants. I hear she's worse than I am." Lionel closes the window.

8

Being a busy and powerful person isn't as sexy as people portray it to be. I haven't been in this position long, but lately, I've been finding it fairly embarrassing. The only reason why I got here is from a conviction I created within myself that I was somehow qualified to convince extraordinarily wealthy people that I was worthy of their investment an investment of their money and, more importantly, their time. Once that investment is received, I then carry that conviction into my circle, where I persuade a series of employees to follow a collection of tasks so that we can achieve some overarching goal. The mere intention behind creating this inner conviction that I am somehow worthy of this influence over others is just embarrassing. I have always been this way. When I was younger I used to prefer to simply lose rather than triggering negative emotions in someone else but things have changed.

    I blindly followed the path of those who appeared to have achieved objective success. But I only realize now it was just created in my mind. But how, and by whom? As I achieved one level, I had already conceptualized the next one. Your environment changes, a new hierarchy appears, and your mood stays the same. Once you climb the highest mountain, you can see a new one appears right behind it, making the one you just climbed horrifyingly irrelevant. The process of climbing then becomes the goal. It's a good goal, too, as long as you ignore just how severely relative goals really are. Your awareness of freedom and how you define it at an early age has an overwhelming effect on the outcome of one's life. But how the hell can I complain? I still don't have any real responsibilities or problems outside of the ones I seem to share with everyone else. Though being a wealthy artist out in the tropics would be much nicer.

What I do is provide a vision for those who can't create one for themselves. I describe fiction to conjure things that will generate wealth and acclaim for all involved. To bridge an idea from fiction to reality, one must understand how to lead an idea. If someone describes an idea with excessive detail, it'll leave little room for people to feel that they can contribute to it, therefore failing to gain the requisite attention of those you seek to attract. Conversely, if an idea is too vague, people will fail to see where and how they can contribute to it. Leadership is, therefore, the ability to summon a vision of the future while maintaining the essential balance of the principal idea when persuading others of its precedence. Lagom is a Swedish word that describes this most closely, as it translates roughly to "just the right amount." My intuition, for whatever reason, is more concerned with discovering the balance of ideas rather than how I can technically engineer the creation of it. It's just one of the many skills that allow individuals to transcend the traditional paths or the socioeconomic hierarchies of the day. A talent for pattern recognition matched with the ability to be aware of the right things at the right time while invoking a force of personality that allows one's fluid articulations to be heard is fundamentally what differentiates. Not the specialization in any one skill. Specialization creates the illusion of creative expression as their skill can only be contributed to the original vision of those paying your bills. You may play the saxophone or the violin better than anyone, but at the end of the day, you will just become a part of someone else's composition. That is why intangible skills will always be more valuable than tangible ones because, ultimately, if you can't define or articulate what makes something valuable, you can't replace or replicate it. What inspires leads, and only truly rare abilities inspire. But what is it worth becoming rare if you can't then live authentically?

Right now I'm heading to get brunch at Captain Blue with my business partner Sam. I've known Sam since we were children. He grew up with unusually strict Russian parents in San Mateo, California. They weren't strict in the traditional sense. Meaning, they didn't care about his grades and usual shit like that. His father was an anarchist and forced his son to learn JavaScript and Go by his fifteenth birthday. His mother was obsessed that Sam dated the most attractive girls at school and won every wrestling tournament. He eventually won a state title in his sophomore year of high school just to get his mother off his back, quitting immediately after. Sam, though somewhat good-looking, always dated the girls out of everyone's league. The other parents and teachers had no idea what to make of them.

As for me I grew up in a broken home with a couple of siblings. We talked about moving a lot, and my parents were always on and off. But starting at around age twelve, I didn't feel a part of it. They always tried to recreate experiences we never had and loved to dream about potential futures as if time were an unlimited resource. After grade school, I lived in a loft above Sam's garage. I wasn't necessarily talented at anything, but most things came quickly to me. Although I did enjoy surfing, it was the only thing I could do while skipping class that didn't make me feel guilty. After high school, we pretended to attend Stanford, living in the garage of an older friend of Sam's who was working in the area. We hung out on campus and eventually began throwing the largest and most extravagant parties at the school. We were spending all the money we were making on these parties from an auto trading bot Sam and I had developed. The bot we made was based on a Markov Chain protocol that got leaked from Howard Morgan's inbox. As the popularity of our parties grew, we realized we had an opportunity to exchange invitations for work. So, we successfully turned one of the designated study areas into a programming haven, where we exchanged solid code for invitations. We quickly found ourselves managing a group of fifteen or so programmers who worked tirelessly between classes on the various ideas Sam and I wanted to test. The projects spanned from testing other auto trading bots to business integration software.

After a year or so, Sam and I became obsessed with the idea that we could run a private software company funded solely by government contracts. If we designed something that would improve an essential government system that protected classified information, we would rapidly grow our network, net worth, and influence in the Valley. We built a prototype and shared it with various government agencies by applying it to the relevant SBIR contracts listed by the Department of Defense. So, ultimately, we received funding and made Hanlon Technologies. Eight years later, Sam and I are some of the youngest and most mysterious technology barons in American history.

Walking into Captain Blue, I immediately notice the new accent wall put up next to the hostess stand. It's made with intricate 3D-printed geometric patterns that immediately create a brilliant, hypnotizing effect on everyone walking in. Unfortunately, it was making my and Sam's favorite spot far too popular for our liking, as all the pretty and popular influencer types couldn't help but buzz over to post pictures of themselves in front of it. As I approach the table Sam is sitting at, I immediately notice that, well, he's pissed.

9

Laying underneath Bona's impressive fireplace, I ice my foot while enjoying the warm ginger tea she had prepared. Bona worked long hours underneath her large windows on a variety of tasks. She seemed to be spending the majority of her time emailing and exercising. She would frequently take long calls, doing them while walking the lawn and trails. Getting up as if she had been listening to me think, Bona leaves the room, and I continue to read:

> Modern man sees himself as inherently unique, with characteristics so uncommon that they naturally ascend socially. Their beliefs free them from categorization by avoiding devotion. However, one's inherent talents are a starting place and have little influence on one's results. This philosophy, in function, is a regressive mode of individuality that rejects responsibility and sacrifice. They reject ideology yet mindlessly ascribe to a new yet ill-informed one they often perceive as being countercultural. Instead of conceptualizing a solution, they instead enforce an awareness that the world isn't at its optimal state and choose to target those

responsible for its creation. Modern men have become problem-seeking creatures, preying on the efforts of the solution-oriented. They view history as a series of events influenced by groups of people and not individuals. They flail in the face of great events, seeking to understand them as an effort by tyrannical cultures driven by group identity. However, the Qoros understand that individuals shape reality and that reality itself is malleable.

> *For reality is a liquid gold awaiting to take form, though its sculptor can only be one capable of seeing the gold as a liquid as well as possessing the concentration to visualize its goal.*

The exercise of concentration through meditation is thus monumental to the Qoros. For if man's subconscious cannot be directed to one's needs, man controls nothing. Making the awareness one has of their mind the tool that one wields to summon moments of improving quality. Prayer, too, in its essence, is nothing like what it's usually seen to be—a submission to the divinity bigger than oneself—when it is simply the process of quieting your small body to focus on the even smaller self until they merge back into the vaster self they come from.

> *To all men, free will lies on a continuum of depth defined by the beholder.*

The history of this planet has just one constant that precedes life itself: hierarchy. A hierarchy of energy. Hierarchy to modern man is an illusory conspiracy maintained by traditional thought. But look no further than how man learns. For man learns by mimicry; every man has learned everything through modeled behavior. The intelligent mimic the correct behavior and are informed regarding what is correct through his or her awareness. It is only through the awareness of one's environment that man is truly intelligent. This is the case because the man most aware of his present environment is the one most suited to manipulate it. They are appropriately attuned to the nuanced biological and psychological senses that drive their ascension. For hierarchy must be omnipresent in the nature of man because awareness too is omnipresent and, like free will, lies on a continuum. The Qoros is thus a chameleon of the highest adaptability and views the exercise of regurgitation as oppressive to its goals.

History is significant to the Qoros as it exposes the extraordinary volatility of human beings. Human beings of all races and creeds have conducted themselves in unbelievably blasphemous ways. Acts of hostility against those who simply think, look, and believe differently prove man's inherent limitations at cooperation. Man, in its essence, carries an instinctual desire to compete with his environment, as men, like resources, are limited. The environment, relative to man, is immortal and thus the epitome of what we struggle to achieve. The conceptualization of this behavior has led man to capitalism. Capitalism acknowledges all man's natural traits more closely than its alternatives, as men are unequal, competitive, and restless. Therefore, to organize men and women toward a collective development, systems of codependency, grounded in the individual, must be preserved. However, it must also possess the capacity to adapt and accommodate itself to the day's needs. Whether that be recalibrations in value structures or definitions of success, our socioeconomic systems possess the capacity to evolve with a culture. For all its wrongdoings, the West has brought the world tools of profound magnitude while improving its ability to offer equality of opportunity to all in its reach. This is the result of a constant tension that exists between commercialization and art which remains the fuel to American life, a life that is constantly testing harmonizations between the ethereal and the practical. To reject and seek the West's eradication at this moment is to seek the suppression of human potential.

Today, there is a war against excellence in our culture. Yet the traditions our civilization poorly protects continue to drive us forward despite their malignant inefficiencies. For man must foresee what the West is approaching: a world of adventure and automation enabled through a revolution of spirit, a revolution outside the limitations of the body and the three-dimensional sensory experience. To discover the next energy medium to harness, we must travel outside ourselves. Our next discovery will lead us to oneness, a life free from the illusion of other.

Fire gave us the earth. Air gave us the sea.
To reach infinity, we must be free to see
Past the "me" toward the "we."

Man has its fingertips on the final frontier to expand and explore infinite planes of existence within and outside our material forms, becoming the Gods we human beings have conceptualized throughout time and across cultures. All peoples throughout history have offered an interpretation of God, but the West differentiated itself by conceptualizing a path to become its equal. Theosis, and most especially the Ubermensch, unlocked an archetypal framework for the post-religious world, providing a new story for man where meaning is found through leading divine action by enforcing God's judgment.

Until the Qoros discovers the next set of objective values that integrates human beings with human life, the Qoros will exist. For we have become the Gods our lesser descendants have forced upon us. At this time, we must offer more radical avenues for consciousness to expand so that we may push, but, more importantly, protect, our collective potential, one that places man in a constant state of becoming. For our civilization to survive this oceanic age, we must integrate our beliefs and behaviors individually and collectively. We human beings remain psychotic in groups due to a lack of collective intentionality, intuition, and compassion—a lack of collective stillness, silence, and peace. Therefore, despite their relevant truths, these modes of being can no longer operate as our ideal conceptualization of what man must worship. To do so would be to worship a present self and not a new ideal. This ideal seeks to use technology to work in symbiosis within its environment. To support the disadvantaged and to decrease the requirements for individual work without centralizing power within too few institutions. This ideal values goodness and cooperation between peoples over everything else.

The next generation of human beings and the innovation that creates them will prioritize expanding sensory experience and time perception.

The civilizations that value the relationship individuals develop with their minds will have the upper hand in this development, for they understand that creating and exploring alternative focal points of consciousness will push the limits of perception and awareness for our collective human mind. We will, therefore, educate our children to develop a relationship with their minds and bodies before encouraging them to pursue any specialization. For the Qoros, formal education environments serve as havens for modern man's ignorance. Today, conventional education constricts creativity, critical thinking, and individuality. Modern men need to gain the skills to identify injustice within the institutions they work and live within. Education no longer challenges our preconceptions. It reinforces them, shaping the ostensibly elite into feeble pawns unconscious of the greater game.

As a consequence, they surrender their being to lifelong debts, guaranteeing themselves as a slave to their oppressor. These modern men take on this debt for the possibility of gaining their oppressor's acceptance. This circumstantial acceptance could facilitate income handed down to them in exchange for *tedious* exercise. Indeed, for modern man to choose this path rationally, he must be ignorant of the path of the Qoros. For if not, he would experience no satisfaction in alcohol, emotionless intimacy, and cursory conversation.

This ignorance can be attributed to a lack of tragedy during adolescence. Grievous events during one's formative years effectively produce highly aware individuals, as the earlier a child encounters something disastrous, the sooner it is aware of its own ignorance. From then on, if the child is so adept, it will seek out this state of being to familiarize itself with it, to become comfortable in it. As this child grows and becomes accustomed to conflict, a new awareness approaches its psyche, an awareness evolved to identify those who have and have not followed this path. This awareness is that of the Qoros, who consult individuals as educators and swear to lifelong self-education. They selectively choose their friends and mentors with rigid preconditions so that their growth may be shared with those capable of absorbing it. Thus, all Qoros are autodidacts who wander their curiosity unfastened while holding zero fear for the tools that elevate that desire.

Though the mind is the greatest tool of the Qoros, his body is treated for what it is: a temporary, decaying vehicle that requires divine treatment. The Qoros, through physical exertion, tests his mind's true potential. For it is only through the body can a Qoros test the will he holds toward his goals. This is the case in societies that address your basic needs with abundance. Under these conditions, new struggles manifest. The struggle of temptation traps men in self-imposed cages due to their lack of a higher calling, a calling that propels you and your progeny to higher spiritual planes.

For modern men habitually consume, linger, and assert. They fail to grow because to do so would require vulnerability, struggle, and reflection. For their only true purpose is to maintain a persona that simulates a sense of equality to their superior. Their superior, however, is habituated to swimming oceans and running mountains. Thus, becoming an extension of nature's selection, the Qoros exposes the great insecurities of modern men with an offhand elegance. They rapidly dissect their persona as the Qoros simply recognize their pernicious attachment to identity. Achievements and failures exist only in the past, but to these men, they are omnipresent, one with their identity. After all, an identity to a Qoros is too adaptable to be besieged. The Qoros, because of his love for the unknown, rapidly metamorphosizes his sense of self, making achievements and criticism from others trivial. For goals are incremental checkpoints to a greater, multigenerational purpose unlikely to be experienced in a time as brief as an individual's life. The briefness of life in relation to the potential multigenerational impact it may have should create deep fear, anxiety, and shame in all men.

But where do the minds of men land when confronted by fear? That nauseating feeling in the pit of your stomach that squeezes the entirety of your being. That pain that forces you to see yourself for exactly what you are at that moment. For after that squeeze, you will never be the same, and through elevating your awareness, you will let go, becoming free from the suffering. Therefore, the awareness of mortality feels no pain as pain but as a triumphant shedding. For this awareness and this feedback is the word of God to the Qoros. It is the kingdom of conscious.

The world itself is the ultimate competition. For a conflict with it would surely bring defeat, but the lessons that inevitably come hold intelligence of the greatest magnitude. That knowledge can then be passed down and ingrained into an inevitably superior progeny. That is why one must understand both technical and practical truths. Information and data broaden the bias of the Qoros. While stored knowledge is accumulated by applying information through as many biases as possible, the individual who conducts this exercise inevitably climbs social hierarchies as he is more successful in communicating with people across social classes. However, as one's knowledge becomes increasingly refined, one's frustration with the less-curious accumulates, straining one's desire to grow further. The Qoros, by its nature, rejects those who regurgitate cultures' prevailing values to extort fame and fortune. These vultures are the oppressors of man. When they identify weakness, they seek to exploit it, not rectify or restore it. The Qoros do not seek to control man but to levy the ones who do. Those seeking to control the herd of mankind are only the weak and insecure who resist the path of the Qoros. These modern men are great enemies to fundamental progress due to their inability to claim ignorance. For the Qoros know most that they know nothing and that knowing anything of true value can only be discovered by confronting what you've left uncharted, a never-ending process of discovery that strengthens the will of man toward gratitude in all things and away from resentment, as resentment is the opposite of gratitude. The relationship between gratitude and resentment drives all relationships—relationships with yourself and others. The accumulation of either is inevitable, so one must be vigilant against the resentments that unconsciously or consciously accumulate. The resentments you store are sinful not because of the thoughts themselves but because of the space they occupy, for every resentful thought represents a rigid wall between yourself and the divinity of your nature. It is your moral duty to preserve a channel of mind that is pure and open.

For a muddied mind will have little ability to acknowledge or appreciate outside forces of lightness or darkness. The modern human condition inevitably leads to conflict, entertainment, and passion. You will be tested forever; the more lightness and pureness you can achieve, the more you will be preyed upon. But to serve those worth serving, you must preserve a prolific openness of mind so that your being serves as a channel for things far greater than yourself, for the things you can't see, hear, smell, or touch. These channels allow you to discover new paths that can bring you a brighter version of your experience, a version that will never leave you. But to open these channels requires a confrontation with precisely the things you are avoiding.

> *For action creates the "how," and our collective destiny lies in doing—in doing the things we fear most by clearing the mind of the dams that seek to limit and protect it.*

The conception of this philosophy represents a moment when man considered themselves worthy of the power they perceived their Gods possessing, as Gods themselves in their most simple interpretation represent a mode of consciousness free from limitation. However, what is a limitation? The limitations we can conceptualize only involve that which our senses allow us to. For a human being itself embodies the ultimate example of survivorship bias. We don't know what we don't know, and we no longer possess the ability to die before we die. But how does one die before they die? You must leave yourself in the most literal sense and experience your consciousness outside your body. This allows each human being to discover their indisputable, inherent divinity. Their immortality. But to achieve this requires divine perception and an absolute integration with one's environment.

To modern men, a God is either something to reject altogether or to accept through faith. Yet, the rejection of God and its blind acceptance are equal failures. For what kind of rational faith can a man have in a God designed by men of lesser descent? A faith that requires conviction based on a poor deposition is an ideology that seeks to restrain, to control. However, rejecting any interpretation of a creator dismisses too many truths. Our world, through nature, suggests that the path to God requires sacrifice. Therefore, communication with God can only be achieved through theosis. To manifest this path, men must revive the ancient path of the Qoros. For the Qoros represents all of what former conceptions of God failed to: a model of behavior that transcends hierarchy, an eye of Horus that harmoniously carries individuals toward selflessness, courage, and love.

The world continues to preserve a ruling class that evaluates the world through a dualistic dogma—heaven and hell, them vs. us, a naive perceptual framework for reality that absorbs all the world's stories and myths. This passive acceptance of dualism constrains the minds of men to an unknowable degree. The writers of these holy books claimed that all beliefs that challenged theirs were motivated by the opposite of what they are, an opposite so evil and powerful that it has halted man from adapting its religious ideas for thousands of years. For "they" must become "us," and "I" must become "we." The Qoros thus rejects all stories which seek to shallow the true nature of reality. The true nature of oneness as reality to a Qoros represents layers of multidimensions far too complicated for binary interpretations. Scientific thinking coupled with secular society has served as a bridge toward a greater understanding of our physical reality, though it is inherently plagued by egotism and groupthink, as science today fails to offer a method for disciplining individuals, a method that tests their commitment to correct study over predictive funding. Therefore, to optimize the progress of science, new metaphysical pioneers must redirect their innovation away from exploitation of nature and toward the elevation of consciousness. To recalibrate science accordingly, new visions for God must be embraced by the minds of the majority. For at this moment, there exists no greater goal. The powerful, the poor, the wealthy, and the abused all require a salvation of the spirit. But how one properly pursues such a goal is in and of itself illusory.

The effort one places toward these goals guarantees nothing without sound awareness of what your environment incentivizes you to do. All great efforts are met with greater abstention and irrational critique. The greater the pursuit, the more excellent the resistance. Only through his awareness can a Qoros traverse these obstacles faithfully. This is difficult, as conscientious men are devastatingly sensitive to community vilification. The more sensitive and caring the leader, the healthier the society. A sign of a sick society requires its leaders to be cold and emotionless. This is our society today, as leaders in every sector of our socioeconomic systems are now required to embody nonlinearity—a mode of sociopathy designed to function amid chaos and controversy. Thus, man requires the empowerment of a new kind of leadership, one more in tune with a classical divine femininity coupled with a masculine persistence and courage. We need kings who are only capable of fighting in the front and queens powerful enough to keep the fighting from happening at all. For our future depends more on an aligned intuition than another conventionally educated manipulator.

10

I put the papers down, notice the sun setting, and begin to make my way outside. Wandering around the porch, I see for the first time how expansive Bona's property is. It appears that this is more of a facility than a home. Flanking the front and back doors of the cabin are two identical buildings. Both are the same in size and design. The one near the back of the house has a large satellite on its roof and is eerily loud by consequence of some sort of sophisticated cooling system. The other, Bona spent much of her time in what appeared to be a gym of sorts, as she would almost always be drenched in sweat upon coming back into the house. As I make my way around the porch, I find Bona and sit with her as she reads her untitled book.

"This is quite an interesting spot, Bona. It must have taken a great deal of time and money to get it set up. I'd happily help you maintain it once my leg heals up. Speaking of, is there anything you have lying around that could help speed up this healing process? Laying around and reading is good and all, but it's beginning to get on my nerves."

Bona closes her book, looks up at me with great intention, and says, "Sure, follow me." We begin to make our way to the building behind the cabin. It's a warehouse with nothing particularly unique apart from the large steel sliding doors. The doors are automatic and can only be opened by a PIN code that Bona neglects to share with me.

The old clunking sound of the mechanism that pulls the doors is satisfying and reminds me of the steampunk video games from my youth. Upon entering the building, one immediately notices a gym-designated area and a grappling mat. Weight vests, kettlebells, and free weights are sprawled across the room. Thick, old ropes hang from the ceiling. The room smells like old sweat, the forest, and maybe some concoction of essential oils. Leaving the room, we take a left into a highly illuminated hallway. The walls are bare, but one door is very much out of place from the otherwise dull concrete and chrome hallway. The door is cherry wood and holds a traditional golden lever handle. We walk up to it, and to my surprise, it serves as an entrance to an elevator. Upon entering this dimly lit box, Bona presses a covered button, sending us down to another one of Bona's inexplicable mysteries. The elevator begins moving, and the dimly lit yellow light suddenly turns into a comforting rose color. In the upper left corner of the elevator is a security camera with a magnifying feature that I can hear inspecting me. I simply smile and wave to it, with Bona visibly disappointed.

All of a sudden, Bona begins to speak. "Listen, Julius. Life is ultimately an experience of limitation. You are either constantly discovering and pushing your limitations forward, or you are beginning to deteriorate." We walk out of the elevator into a room dimly lit with the same rose color. The room has only one freezer and a small, highly raised door. Bona pauses, regaining my attention, and continues to speak. "People generally understand this in terms of physical limitations. Society is obsessed with stories of people who are tremendously skilled physically and fundamentally symbolize our Darwinian progressions. Any overcoming of physical adversities in the form of injuries or diseases by athletes and soldiers are glorified extensively. However, what fascinates me and the people who you seem to want to connect with is the inseparable relationship between mind, body, and…something else. Call it God, your spirit, soul, whatever. But I can guarantee that you will not get terribly far if you do not develop a rigid faith in this third quality."

She walks over to the freezer and grabs a small vial and needle.

"Creating habits every day that sharpen these three dimensions of self is required for people like you and me to experience any sort of fulfillment. So, one of the best ways to do that is to meditate in this."

She opens the small high-rise door, pulling a large latch that you often only see on a large walk-in freezer, and gestures to me to reach inside. It's dark and humid. I reach around and feel a warm pool of water with a particularly dense composition.

"This chamber is soundproof, resistant to all light, and the water automatically adjusts to your body temperature. The water is a simple mix of Epsom salts and a redox-signaling molecule solution. Here, you experience none of your senses and therefore witness reality in a way you haven't since you were inside your mother. If you can calm your mind here, do what I tell you to do, and take what I ask you to take, I promise that your leg and therefore your mind will heal much more quickly."

She signals for me to take a seat on the floor, begins rolling up the leg of my pants on the side of my injured ankle, and abruptly stabs the needle into my lower calf. "These are stem cells derived from the placenta of an unusually healthy young woman I used to know." Holding back any sign of pain, I nod my head, displaying an all-too-pointless approval. Bona then heads back to the freezer, grabs another small vial, and hands it to me. This one has strange symbolic markings, the ones I had seen in the hallway. The vial has a peculiar reflective quality and is sealed with an orange cap.

"Now Julius, this is lusis. It's a tincture with psychedelic qualities that you're going to take before getting in there," she says, signaling toward the tank. "It guides the body into a state of sleep paralysis. Once your body is completely asleep, lusis will fire dormant energy from the base of your spine into the crown of your head. This sensation will give you the opportunity to remain completely conscious while the body is asleep. It takes about an hour or two to set in and lasts for about six hours, so you're going to be in there for a while, and I can't let you out until it's over. Also! No food or water until you're done. Any questions?"

"Are you kidding, Bona? How do you expect me to trust you, take this random thing I've never heard of, and then hop into this wet coffin just because you said so? What is in this anyway?" I asked, shoving the vial toward her face.

"Well, it's mostly composed of things you've never heard of, but there is a little bit of mescaline and synthetic ibogaine if you've heard of those things. It doesn't really matter, and it's not like you have a choice anyhow. But once you feel your cerebrospinal fluids firing, make sure you keep it moving. You can't get terribly far if not."

"Why are you talking to me as if I have any idea what you are talking about?" Fortunately for me and my personality, I am more curious than afraid of what Bona is proposing.

I sigh and ask, "So, when should we get started?" Bona smiles and hands me a bottle of water. "Pound this down, and afterward, you'll just drink this little vial and hop inside whenever you're ready." Walking toward the elevator, Bona stops, looks over her shoulder, and says, "Julius?"

"Yes, Bona?" I say nervously.

"Just be sure to focus on your breath and try not to focus on your leg. I'll be tracking you from upstairs. Good luck."

Clueless as to how I should appropriately respond, I nod earnestly at the camera that pointedly sits atop the elevator. Now alone in this strange, dimly lit room, I begin to feel my heartbeat pick up. I'm unsure if I've ever been this nervous, but I try not to dwell on it. I slow my breath to help calm myself, chug the water, and take a moment to pray the most general prayer. In my mind, I ask for a guide to watch over and protect me from what is to come. Feeling more relaxed, I stand up and touch my toes to stretch for a moment before entering the chamber.

I unscrew the cap of the bottle and smell the liquid inside. It's salty and seems to be based in a familiar oil. I take it back and begin stripping down my clothes. I feel the urge to be completely nude, thinking I'd be more comfortable that way inside. Pulling the latch, I turn around, smile, and wave puckishly to the camera in the corner of the room as I climb inside. Closing the door behind me, I begin feeling for a handle. To my dismay, I feel a hole in the place the handle would be and mentally curse Bona for exacerbating an already onerous collection of conditions. Returning to my breath, I lay down in the water and am immediately surprised by the buoyancy and darkness of the chamber. Unfortunately, as I lengthen out, I notice that I am too tall for the confined space and have to lie diagonally so as not to have my head or feet touch the sides. I settle myself again and begin to meditate.

The air here is humid and more difficult to breathe than the mountain air I was getting accustomed to. I feel it loosening my sinuses and other areas of pressure around my face. In some areas, I wasn't conscious of possessing any tension at all. For the first forty-five minutes, laying in the water feels like a physical therapy session. Slowly, my body eases as the chemicals in the water begin reacting with my skin. But just as my body relaxes fully, an unfamiliar pressure begins to mount on my injured foot. Quickly, almost exponentially, the pressure turns to pain, and the pain turns to complete horror. In a fit of panic, I scream and start hyperventilating. I'm in a full-blown panic attack and can't calm myself, splashing in the water. I let out another scream and pray for Bona's presence. I scream out, "BONA! HELP ME…MY FOOT, MY FOOT!" The pain only gets worse, and I begin to feel dazed, as if close to fainting. I then feel the sensation in my spine that Bona has described and start taking the deepest breaths I can while forcing my eyes open to stay conscious. I'm in and out and begin to grow even more full of fear.

But then I notice it as just that—I'm afraid. But afraid of what? The pain? The isolation? Drowning? Yes, all risks I voluntarily brought into this moment, into my life. I distract myself and begin focusing my attention on why this is happening for me and not to me. Staying on this wavelength of thought, I begin to feel the pain release ever so slightly.

After what I suspect to be a couple of hours, the pain slowly begins leaving my body as I am enveloped in a nauseating euphoria. I find my way back to my mantra, "Let go and grow," and my breath and nervous system begin to steady. Little orbs and glitches, like cue marks at the movies, start jumping in and out of my mind's eye. My body then begins to vibrate at a meager and anxiety-inducing pace. I feel as if I am sinking, like something is being extracted from below me. Seeking to quiet my mind further without using the mantra, I am introduced to a translucent-colored marquise. I seek to differ my attention from it in an effort to keep it with me, and to my surprise, it stays, fluttering in a peculiarly seductive fashion, embodying a new yet familiar energy.

For some time, I rest with it, making it my companion. The sinking and lowering vibration has slowed, easing my meditational efforts. Suddenly, the marquise-shaped presence begins to pulse and distort, forcing my body to follow. My breath is shortened, and my body twitches despite the numbness. The shape then begins rapidly replicating and folding over itself until settling into what can only be described as a powerful, angelic wing. Almost filling my vision, the wing shakes, sending me deeper into a now wholly unfamiliar territory, one full of satisfaction and love, yet free from the possessive or lustful undertones. I feel a tear run down the right side of my cheek as the being reveals himself, looking over his angelic shoulder just for a moment. A sudden flash transforms my vision from a dark void into a blinding field. The focal point of my consciousness becomes increasingly concentrated in its position. It begins to lift, almost propelling itself away from my physical form. At first, the sensation is healing and clarifying, allowing me to enter the most profound states of awareness more quickly than I have ever achieved. But as I go deeper, the concentration of my focal point begins to create a deep pressure. The pressure starts to mount, and my eyes begin flashing rapidly. I know this experience Bona set me into is just beginning.

I wake up on the floor in my room in California. It's dusk, and the room is unusually hazy. My body feels like every muscle has fallen asleep, and I cannot move. I try to stand, but I fail and begin to crawl toward the door. As I move, I feel as if I am being pushed downward into the floor. I finally reach the door and awkwardly force it open. Upon opening it, I see that I am not where I thought I was. Expecting my living room, I see miles of what can only be described as

Armageddon. There is nothing but ash and metal buildings crumbling into nuclear craters. The radioactive fumes force me unconscious.

I awaken on the floor again, at the same spot, and in the same condition. My impulse again is to make my way toward the door. So, I crawl toward it and open it. It is my house, but it appears to have been abandoned for decades. The carpets are moldy, the windows are broken, and the furniture is gone. Perplexed, I try to enter the room, but I go unconscious.

I awaken again on the floor, at the same spot, and in the same condition. I begin to feel overwhelmed and unsure of myself, so I crawl toward the door again. As I get closer, a small hideous creature appears in the corner of my ceiling. The creature has a long nose and pointy ears. Its eyes are a sharp green color and are difficult to look at.

In a whisper, it asks me, "Why are you going toward the door again? I don't think you're going to find anything you like."

Hearing the creature's words and crackling laughter makes me feel sick. It is as if just hearing them is poisoning my mind and body. My capacity to reason my way out of the situation is severely constrained as it becomes increasingly difficult to think clearly. My mind becomes more clouded, and the room increasingly dark. I then begin to feel a lifting sensation from above me. My body begins to rise, and I'm in and out of consciousness. The lifting settles and now I am in a blindingly lit room and am no longer alone. My eyes are covered, and all I can hear are strange murmurs and jittery scurrying around me. They are attaching various devices to me, and I begin to grow anxious again, but I cannot defend myself or even think in language. An overwhelming sense of fear washes over me. The scurrying around me becomes more chaotic until the lights in the room go out, sending my unknown company into a frenzy of screams. The screams are incredibly high-pitched, worsening my state. I am now at a level of fear I have never come close to experiencing before.

Abruptly, I am grabbed and pulled down back into my room and then pulled through the floor. Everything goes dark. I am now stuck in a cold pit wrapped in a scaldingly hot web. I'm on my stomach, and a tremendous weight begins resting itself on my back. There's heavy breathing down my neck and claws tearing into my waist. Afraid to look at what's on top of me, I close my eyes and hear an evil whisper say, "Hello, Julius. What makes you think you can be here?" He begins groping me up and down, pushing my energy lower and sending me in and out of consciousness. His grip on the back of my neck tightens while his claws slowly tear my skin. He shows his demonic self to me in my mind's eye briefly, sending my vibration further down.

Freefalling and no longer able to hear my thoughts, I begin to realize what is happening. I begin seeking new ways of increasing my vibration without conscious thought. Feeling my way to something I can hold in my mind, I find a forgotten place, a place I used to escape to when I was a child—a clearing in the woods behind our house where I'd often go alone to do rituals with my blades and collected stones. The clearing was created by a large rock formation, making it impossible for any tree or plant to grow. I explore every detail of the fulgent green sanctuary and begin to feel the demon's grip loosen. My body is drawn inward, and with every gain in vibration, I fold inward until all that is left is a translucent marquise. Out of nowhere, I disappear into a tunnel of magnificent orange rings. The rings pulse in sync with my frequency and demand an incredible amount of energy. The rings begin to dissolve into white as I enter my final effort.

I awaken in an expansive field pronounced by subtle glowing hills. The grass isn't coarse. It's gentle. It triggers none of the senses in my feet as I walk across it. I feel I am in a much less rigorous physical environment. My movement is graceful. My breathing requires no effort. As I stroll through this blank space, I notice the feedback from my environment as I breathe. It's breathing with me, moving with me and feeling with me. I begin to manifest everything I picture in my mind instantaneously. Skyscrapers zip into the sky. Bright gardens slither in parallel with an expanding babbling brook. Great monoliths showcasing the symbols in Bona's hallway rise. As I walk, I create. As I create, I am heard by the things that remain my superior. A tiny lamb elegantly appears and scurries up toward the landscape's tallest hill. I follow, and as I approach its peak, a sprawling fig tree begins to grow. The lamb dances by its base, and I sit beneath it and start to quiet my mind.

After several breaths, the orange rings reappear, and I feel my body concentrate and fold into itself. The frequency I created internally is refashioned into a sort of vehicle. I fly through some middle dimension, dancing between the intermediaries of space and time using my consciousness to travel unfastened through a multiverse—a space where the energy you create internally is immediately reflected externally. Suddenly, the rings disintegrate, and I appear again in complete darkness.

I hear murmuring around me. I try to move but I can't get up. I am trapped inside of some small metal box. I push the walls around me, and there is no give. I push the top of the box with my back and feel it move ever so slightly. I force through it and am on a podium. A wave of gasps erupts through the room. I'm in some kind of chapel full of individuals whose bodies are in a similar form as my own. They are subtly golden, and everyone but me is wearing a heavy blue cloak. Behind a large altar where a priest-like figure is presenting is a window. Through it, to my amazement, Earth. A tall, thin man with dark, splintering eyes is on the far side of the black and gold metal cube from which I arose. The moment I make eye contact with him, I fall to my knees as the intensity of his stare knocks me instantly, draining me. He looks at me with a great combination of anger and intrigue. Suddenly, a hooded girl lifts me and crisply whispers, "You're not supposed to be here." She runs me down the aisle away from the podium, holding my hand as the others pursue us. We run into a hexagonal corner of the room and vanish, appearing in a wild environment with purple skies, riding horseback in a full gallop. We make eye contact, and we appear under a giant wave. As the wave crashes on us, we reappear on the roof of a skyscraper. Ahead of me, she runs off the roof and flies away. I follow, but as I jump, I fall and wake up back in the chamber at Bona's.

"Bona! Bona! I'm back!"

Through the intercom, Bona responds, "Julius, are you okay? I am coming down now!"

11

"What are you doing tonight?" asks Sam irritably. He often gets restless when he gets too much or too little of something.

"I'm going to see the ballet with Vendhaya," I reply, somewhat apprehensively.

"You and your ballets. Haven't you seen this one?" says Sam, smirking.

"Yes, this will be my second time seeing it. I've told you before. It clears my head. Besides, I like the people there. They aren't as snobby as you like to make them out to be. They're a calm, confident bunch who value the most microscopic progressions. Makes me feel like I'm a more patient person."

"How can you keep a straight face while saying something like that? I thought you were dating someone else?"

"I'm pretty sure Eve ended things this morning. But honestly, I like this Vendhaya girl so far. She's curious, well-educated, and has incredible self-control. Maybe the only woman I've met who I would describe as stoic."

"Self-control?"

"Yeah, she doesn't have sex."

"She doesn't have sex? Like, she's never had sex?" says Sam pointedly.

"She's had sex, but with only a couple of serious boyfriends. She thinks about sex. Sex with me even. She's just one of those people who I imagine can use her mind with such clarity that she can create just about any kind of pleasure for herself. She's shockingly content and pure. It's a shame no one taught her how to use it for something. Aside from, you know…rationalizing why she shouldn't sleep with me."

"You always do this. You find the quietest and prettiest girls and project this totally unwarranted depth onto them. Vendhaya is a rich girl who, like the rest of them, has just romanticized their negative emotions for a creative inspiration they'll never apply to anything."

"That doesn't matter. But I hear you." Noticing the clock ticking over my right shoulder, I feel time begin to pulse irregularly. Easing into the metronomes, I start taking in the subtleties of the restaurant. The posture of the man sitting beside Sam is beginning to crumble as he finally realizes that he is once again feeding another photogenic girl who has zero intentions of pursuing any relationship or intimacy with him. The seascape acrylic paintings across the room are lined with thin steel frames that reflect the handbags and watches of the people who enter the restaurant. A middle-aged woman who is always starting something new sits at the window with her small dog, looking through the glass thoughtlessly. She is a material monk, completely still, only able to envision the next four-figure trinket she will purchase. Then, a skinny kid with a pointless Nikon camera walks in with another heart collector. She poses by the accent wall as the kid's camera flashes through the restaurant.

"It's tragic…people continue to be possessed by this micro-celebrity nonsense—phony self-expression. We are social creatures, sure. We do need to satisfy that part of ourselves but, turning yourself into that"—Lionel points to the posing girl—"can at best get you what? Attention, status-driven sex, cleaner drugs?"

"I don't care. I don't value self-expression," says Sam. "If it's so valuable, why is it so abundant? You can't escape it. The attention addicted…men, women, gay, fat, fit, doesn't matter. They all seek to have people dependent on them so they can help weaker people in the ways they think is best. But it's not self-expression itself. It's the model they are forced into. It's just an experimental trial and error between you and a sick world, a world disconnected from any meaningful purpose. A world so sick that it forgot why and how it became the way it is. Human beings follow, but celebrities are the worst kind of followers. They follow the masses. Actors dressed like generals."

"Very poetic," says Lionel jokingly.

"Oh, come on. You know what I mean. We all have our vices, but it's important to point out the ones that everyone blindly shares—especially the ones we share across classes. An addiction to attention is just one of those things. I'm not trying to make it out to be better or worse than any other addiction. It just is what it is. We all need vices, because our individual pursuits can only take us so far. None of us have a community. We really are the spiritual orphans you like to talk about. By the way, I've been using that thing you gave me. It's unbelievable, man. I can't stop using it. I need more time with it."

"No way, we have a deal! We take turns with this thing, and it's my turn," says Lionel pointedly.

"How come we can't get more of it anyway?"

"Because I stole the goddamn thing, and I haven't told anyone else about it besides you. I was thinking about getting Ming to look at it, but then we couldn't use it. I need it back."

"Fine, I need to get out and socialize anyway. And how the hell did you steal this thing?" says Sam curiously.

"I was surfing at Cortes Bank on the boat. I was loaded up on some phenibut and drank a little too much. As the jet ski pulled me in, this exotic superyacht came from nowhere and anchored itself. I was invited on the boat, and we partied together, but everything from there was a blur. I remember they were all somehow too beautiful for me not to recognize them. I also met Vendhaya there. But other than that, I woke up in the morning with that suitcase by my bed. Do you have it with you?"

Sam stands up. "William picked it up fifteen minutes ago. I should be getting out of here. I'm not hungry, and I need to catch up on some stuff. Have fun with that," says Sam as he leaves the restaurant.

12

I'm with William, driving aimlessly through Manhattan. I contemplate whether I should continue my rigorous schedule or open this briefcase. Inside, there are these brilliant translucent bottles. Each bottle has an orange cap that can't get screwed on again once it is removed. The bottle's material seems extraterrestrial and doesn't remind me of any material I have seen before. The bottle inverts the light that reflects off its surface, creating miniature prisms within it. The mere sight of the briefcase is intoxicating. I grew to love the ritual of opening the suitcase with its firm, mechanical switches. Fidgeting with the bottles and unscrewing the cap has become ceremonious. Up until this point, I have only had the courage to take a little less than half of a bottle. Taking just half a bottle allows me to stay conscious and step inside a wonderful version of reality that I couldn't access without it.

"William, you can drop me off here. I'm just going to wander around the city between now and the dance tonight. Just tell anyone who asks that I had to fly to Washington."

Stepping out onto a random street, I take down half the vial and hand the rest to a homeless man sitting in a surprisingly complex cardboard fortress. Walking around the city always makes me feel calm. I used to hate the feeling of being a part of the herd, but now I've grown to appreciate it. The collective ignorance is more comforting than my elitist isolation.

I love to pretend I don't overtly feel this sense of not knowing, this sense that there is something behind everything. Both directly and indirectly, I feel that invisible strings orient the masses toward some sort of docile mediocrity, that me and everyone else is being kept in the dark. This "they" are able to satisfy our minds and bodies, but that third dimension, the dimension of spirit, is starving and desperate for attention. This tremendous spiritual void exists in us, rich or poor, healthy or sick, deformed or beautiful. The spiritual suffering exists across classes, races, cultures, and borders. There is nothing meaningful that we can all agree to believe in.

We need a spiritual leader, but our society has grown fearful of great individuals and become convinced that revolutions can now manifest peacefully via decentralized leadership. We have too many ideas and too many problems to gain any collective clarity. It is this spiritual suffering that eats at us, not political or economic injustices of race or class. But we continue to fight against each other, not the ideas we unquestioningly embrace. But what can any one person do when no one knows where power truly lies? Where is power safeguarded? Why do they feel so safe from us that they never need to show themselves?

I turn the corner into an alley and notice a happy couple walking down a staircase. Intrigued, I follow, waiting momentarily for the door to close behind the glowing pair. As they open the door, the steam on the floor lifts into the alley, flagging the decadence that likely takes place inside. Walking in, the room is unusually dark, with green lamps and candles sparse throughout the urban labyrinth. The first room I enter has a bar with two men dressed in red jumpsuits serving drinks. I hop on one of the stools and notice I have begun to feel the chemicals enter my bloodstream. Deep house is playing through the room, successfully masking the normalcy occurring outside.

I ask one of the men at the bar, "What's this place called?"

"We don't have a name. We are only in town for a couple of days. Did you receive an invitation? It's invite only."

"Of course I did," I say quickly. "Just curious if this space was used for something before. Thanks."

Getting up, I light a joint from my pocket and continue to explore the winding hallways. The rooms are incredibly stark and eclectic. The deep green floors and black walls are paired with large, orange polka dot paintings and distorted Moroccan sculptures. I continue down the hall, and someone taps me on my shoulder.

"Lionel? Is that you? What are you doing here?" says an unknown woman fanatically.

"Sorry? I'm not sure I know you. How do you know my name?"

"We met at Cortes Bank; you don't remember? How did you get in here?"

Suddenly, her friend in a red dress approaches me from behind, grabbing my arm. "It's so good to see you, Lionel. I can't believe you're here!"

We make our way down the hall, and I begin to feel lighter. We spread out across a room full of couches wrapped in green velvet. They pour champagne and begin telling me stories about when I was drinking on the boats. I pretend to listen, enjoying the decadence that my luxurious youth enables. Suddenly, three prominent men walk in, and the girls almost instantly disappear. The men are dressed in obscure, heavy black clothing. One with long hair sits on the couch in front of me while the other two stand intensely behind.

"Who are you?" asks the now-obvious leader sitting across from me.

"Don't you recognize me? My name's Waldo. You deserve my congratulations."

"You look good, Lionel. Why do those girls know you?" the man says sternly over the music.

"Just met them. I was just getting ready to go actually," I say, standing up.

"Go where? How will you leave?"

"Well, if you guys would let me, I'd happily walk out that door, and we'd never have to see each other again. I didn't mean to disrupt anything you guys had going on here."

"You have no idea where you are. I do know that you somehow got access to something that is very dangerous for you to have. I know you were on our boat not too long ago. I don't know how you got ahold of that briefcase. I don't really care. In fact, I feel sorry for you that you're in this situation."

"I have no idea what you're talking about."

"Don't play games. Why are you treating me as if I'm police? We are way scarier than that, my friend. Tell me. How is it then that I know you're using some right now?"

"Using what? And I'm pretty sure I know exactly where I am."

"Ha, well, you see, you aren't here, because here is nowhere. But if you want to survive, Lionel, you'll need to give me the briefcase the next time I see you. Remember, we three can be anywhere and everywhere at every time."

Suddenly, he claps his hands in my face, and I am thrown forward through the cabin of my car. I look up through the window and see William limp across the steering wheel. He has two bullet holes in his head, and he has just rear-ended the cab in front of him. I get out with the briefcase and start running as fast as possible.

13

A young Vendhaya wakes up and crawls to the sunspot at the other end of her room. Stretching her legs, she looks at the window and sees an emerald moth crawling along the glass. Enthralled, she rushes over to the window to let it in, but as she opens it, the moth begins to soar back into the forest. Vendhaya quickly grabs her shoes and hops out the window, chasing after it. Her mother, Rebecca, calls for her with concern, "V, get back here right now! I need to speak with you." Frustrated, Vendhaya sighs and jogs toward her mother, lying on a large tapestry on the lawn behind their beautiful estate.

"Did you remember to write in your dream journal this morning?"

"No, I got distracted. I didn't really have any dreams anyway."

"Well, did you at least put your phone away and pray a little before bed?"

"No, not really."

"V, that is not safe for us to do. You are leaving yourself way too vulnerable out there. It just isn't safe enough for us to live that way. It's irresponsible."

"I know, Mom. It's scary either way, though, you know? Praying, not praying. Putting my phone away and being alone like that is scary for me."

"I understand; your father used to be the same. But unlike him, you need to remember why you're here and who brought you here. We are all being tested. We are all on the same journey. Did you know in the bible, the most repeated message is, 'Do not be afraid'? Yet all of us still fear. Most people's lives are defined by their inability to face their fears."

"But what do people fear?"

"They fear, fear. They avoid it until they can't. But it is strange, because when we face our fears, we engage in the most important adventures of our lives. That is why dragons sleep on gold. Behind our greatest fears are gifts greater than our imagination can allow."

"Abby's mom thinks that when we dream and use lusis, we actually die."

"No, she doesn't understand. She is still afraid. That is why her children struggle so much."

"What do you mean, she's afraid? What do you think she is scared of?"

"She's afraid of dying, V."

"And you aren't?"

"No. I know what happens when you die."

"No one knows that. Dad says that all the time."

"Well, Vendhaya, I know what happens," Rebecca says cheerfully.

"What happens?"

"When we die, we experience the reality of dying. Our authentic response to that new reality defines what happens next. If you are resentful, regretful, and faithless, your consciousness will incarnate in an environment or a form that matches that vibration. But if you are full of gratitude, authenticity, excitement, and love, you will do the same. That is why you have nothing to fear when you live your life with courage. You see, V, you only have one creator, and you are an energetic being. That creator is the only thing we truly know is real. If you look closely, the ones who do wicked things are those who invert him, invert the love he taught us. They seek to equate what is above with what is below. They believe that what is inside us is no better or different than what is outside of us. They say things like, 'As it is on earth, so it is in heaven. As I am, so are my cells, so are my atoms, and so is God. As I believe the world to be, so it is.' They only accept the first six days because they seek to become Gods themselves. All reflection is rejected. Creation is their North Star, not love. They may appear powerful, but they aren't. All they desire is to have you forget who brought you here so that they can deceive you into accepting the illusion that is their power."

Vendhaya listens intently to her mother's words, her mind swirling with the weight of their meaning. She had always sensed something missing; now, her mother's words confirm it. As she sits on the tapestry beside her mother, Vendhaya gazes up at the vast expanse of blue sky above them. The warm sun kisses their skin, casting a golden glow over the sprawling estate. But amid the beauty, she can't help but feel a sense of unease, like a storm brewing in the distance. "Mom, so are we meant to be here? Or are we meant for something past all this?"

Rebecca's eyes soften as she turns to face her daughter. "Oh, Vendhaya," she whispers. "We are destined for so much more than what we can see. Our journey here is just a glimpse of what awaits us. Here, we are bound to love and experience love in all its forms. But keep in mind, the true nature of love is itself a deception, as loving is the process of bonding and mixing. But to be able to mix, we had to be split—Eve from Adam, electrons from atoms. We were once whole, now we are split. But to start to unmix, we begin to exist. We are all souls split from their whole. That is what lusis allows you to do."

"What do you mean? What does it allow me to do?"

"To become whole again."

14

I finish recalling my experience to Bona. She seems taken aback, even scared.

"You were freediving outside your mind, Julius. A freediver can only explore for as long as they can hold their breath. Similarly, through a deep enough meditative state, you can concentrate your consciousness on a single point. It's a spiritual concentration that allows you to explore reality outside the third dimension. Through that focal point, you can explore reality with far fewer limitations than what one can do through the mind or body. There, reality mirrors itself instantaneously. You are relearning the oneness described by Empedocles and the pre-Socratics. When consciousness removes itself from the body like this, it becomes far more sensitive and takes away your ability to process emotions through language. An ordinary person can typically get a taste of your experience through sleep paralysis, but what you claim to be doing is far more advanced, especially on your first time. You are no longer safe here. We have to leave immediately."

"Why? How can they possibly know we are here? Who are they?"

"The Qoros. They are real. But they are not like the Qoros from those pages. They are different now. You see, Julius, I am the daughter of Neberu Menidys, the man who wrote those pages and initially synthesized lusis."

"Who was he? Where is he now? Can we talk to him?"

"He was a chemist in the '70s and was raised by an Italian military officer, Roh Menidys, and his mother Hirut, who taught ancient antiquities. They met when Roh was sent to Ethiopia to support the Italian military's occupation efforts. However, Roh quickly went rogue and escaped with Hirut to the Namibian coast. There, they raised Neberu on a ranch in rigorous conditions. He was homeschooled and spent his summers hunting with local tribes. He became a chemist and philosopher, eventually moving to America and ultimately synthesized lusis. He chose to share it only with his closest friends, and together, they wrote those pages reviving the Qoros. As they became more skilled with lusis, they developed immense power. They manipulated the psyches of many rich and powerful people, leading them to seize enormous resources. But then things went south, fast. His closest friend Sinil Pilate and the other Qoros betrayed my father when he decided to take lusis to the masses. Sinil and the others wanted to secure their power for themselves and their families, believing humanity was not ready for something so transformative. Tensions rose, and my father escaped on his own back to Namibia. But just as he was completing the construction of his lab, Sinil and the others found him and killed him. Only Sinil, the other Qoros, and their children can produce lusis."

"How is that possible? How is it possible to hide something like this from the world?"

"It's actually quite simple, Julius. Over the past sixty years, America has become a prison colony. We have more people in prison per capita than any civilization in history. And who rises to the top in prison or jail? Who has all the control? It's whoever controls the drugs. Our country is now no different. The Qoros control us because they don't only control lusis but every other pharmaceutical, drug, and medicine. When they discovered lusis, they could quickly produce what is essentially the opposite of it—drugs and medication that stifle our ability to experience anything spiritual."

"So, what do we do?"

"I don't know. I don't even know where that facility in Namibia is. Even if we could find it, they've probably moved it by now."

All at once, a blazing head rush washes over me, and I collapse to my knees.

"Oh no. No, no, no. Julius! The lusis is still in your system. You woke up earlier than you were supposed to."

Bona lays me down on the lawn beside her cabin. "You're going back. Try to look for the facility. Don't stay in one place for too long, and don't let any of the Qoros touch you. I'll be here when you wake up."

My body becomes increasingly numb until I suddenly slip out of my body and through the ground beneath me. My vision goes dark.

15

I appear floating over the ocean. The sun is setting, and I can see the Qoros chapel in the sky.

"You seem to know what you're doing."

I see the hooded girl across from me, elegantly hovering above the calm seas beneath her, her skin a crystallizing golden hue.

"Oh, believe me, I don't have the slightest clue what I'm doing. What's your name?"

"My name is Vendhaya. Yours?"

"Julius."

Vendhaya removes her hood to reveal her straight, elven blond hair. "You're the first stranger I've met here. People will jump out by accident for a moment or two while asleep. But never like you, never like this. Typically, it takes years of training with the Qoros to jump like this."

"Are you Qoros then?"

"I suppose. I was born into it. I don't know anything else. I don't know much about where we come from."

"Why did you save me then?"

"I'm not sure why. I just had a feeling. I was compelled to do it. My mother would have liked you. But you are not safe. My father will do everything he can to stop you from taking lusis ever again. How did you get it?"

"I can't tell you."

"Julius, there are only so many people who could have given it to you, and based on your innocence alone, I'm already fairly certain I know who it is."

"I need to get to Namibia, to the facility."

"Why, to do what? Even if I could get you there, there's nothing you'll be able to do."

"I don't know. I just know I need to find it."

Suddenly, Vendhaya launches herself forward, grabbing my arm, revealing the location of my body.

"I see. You're with Bona in that abandoned compound in the woods; smart. So, your goal is to do what Bona's father intended?"

"Yes. But this is all still new to me. Is Bona's father wrong?"

"I'm not sure. Probably not. But either way, you two aren't going to be able to do this alone. I can't be seen with you."

Vendhaya turns around, getting ready to leave. "Why are you doing this, Julius?"

"I just want to do what's right. I trust Bona. The people in control of you up there aren't good. I've seen their eyes. All they want is control, control over something far too powerful and important. Lusis is what people need; without it, we'll continue to fall and suffer. How is it possible you're able to stand by and just let this happen? Don't you see what this world is becoming?"

"Julius, you need to be careful. It isn't obvious that the average person is ready for this."

"Ready for what? Who is doing the protecting exactly?"

"Listen, I probably do agree with you, but that doesn't mean there is anything I can do about it. A kingdom exists behind your eyes. That is all my father will see when he sees you. That is why you are a threat to him. It isn't the fact that you can soar around like this."

The sky begins to go dark, and Sinil appears and approaches us. His energy is very different from Vendhaya's. Vibrating off of him are static electric forces reverberating off his body. "Go home, V. This boy no longer concerns you. He and I must formally meet."

"Do not hurt him. You can speak to him with me here." Suddenly, two others grab V and jump her back to the chapel.

"Who taught you about us, Julius? I hope you are enjoying this, because this will be your last time jumping. I'll ensure you never get your hands on lusis again."

"What are you trying to control?" I can see the anger in Sinil's eyes as he floats closer to me. His energy crackles around him, creating an invisible barrier of tension between us, though I hold my ground, refusing to let the fear consume me.

"What am I trying to control? The most delicate thing anyone has ever controlled. You do not know what the consequences are. Too naive, too dangerous."

My vision goes black, and I wake up again in my body, looking up at Sinil standing over Bona.

"It's a shame really. She was the last of an actually legitimate competition." Sinil, with his foot, kicks over Bona's limp hand.

Sinil effortlessly forces my body down as I begin to stand by placing his hand on my shoulder. "She put you in a messy situation, didn't she? But honestly, this is all going to work out great for you."

I reach toward his head, trying to grab him, but he is immovable, dragging me along the floor like a small child. Sinil walks me back into the cabin, stepping through the gothic mirror and arriving back to the chapel. We walk into a small room, and he places me on a raised metal platform. The platform automatically straps me to its frame and slides backward into a chamber. As my feet pass through, the chamber seals, and a bright red light floods the space. A robotic voice begins to speak to me from inside my head like a silken serpent slithering through the recesses of my mind. "There, there, Julius. Let go. Let go. No need to squirm. Soon, the web will be gone, and you'll be free."

Julius, caught in the sticky threads of the voice's hypnosis, feels his past dissolving, his identity blurring. "What?" he croaks.

"You are clay," the voice hisses. "Moldable, malleable. I, the potter, shall shape you into something new, something beautiful. For me."

"But what about..." Julius sputters, battling the intensifying numbness.

The voice chuckles, a cold, metallic sound like sheets of ice scraping bone. "Just illusions, Julius. Distractions from your true purpose. Now, you'll serve a higher calling."

"But...my friends..." Julius's voice trails off.

"Chains, Julius. Chains I'll gladly sever. You are reborn not as a man, but as an instrument, a perfect tool."

Julius feels himself surrendering, the terror curdling into a cold, hollow dread. "Then...what am I to become?" he whispers, lost in the abyss that is his mind.

"You," the voice croons in a chilling echo, "will be what we need you to be: a dancing shadow, a whisper of your former self, forever enthralled by the Qoros, the great leaders who now hold your very essence."

Julius erupts in a crushing, guttural moan.

"Shh, Julius. This is just the beginning of your beautiful rebirth."

Metal tendrils, cold and barbed, begin to burrow into his face, scraping away his flesh. Julius writhes, his muscles seizing and spasming, but the straps bind him like a fly in amber. Every twitch, every strangled cry, heard by no one.

"See, Julius," the voice purrs, "your old self was a simple canvas marred by weakness and dissatisfaction. Simply a starting place for who your Gods need you to be."

The tendrils continue to carve. New cheekbones, now sharper and higher, emphasizing the intensity of his eyes. His jawline transforms, becoming a cruel crescent blade jutting forward. Each tear of skin feels like a searing brand. Tiny needles plunge into his eyes, rearranging the irises, etching them with a new shape, new color. His once kind, expressive eyes become dark and severe. Julius's screams finally die in his throat, replaced by a whimpering, ragged sob as the transformation nears its end. The tendrils retreat, leaving behind a face that no longer belongs to him. It is a beautifully sculpted mask, a terrifyingly perfect caricature of a man. And in the suffocating silence, Julius lets go. The memories, the fears, the very spark of his individuality bleed away, leaving behind a hollow shell. He is nothing.

Vendhaya barges into the room, watching Julius's chamber shoot out of the chapel and toward Earth. "You monster! How dare you? What did he do to deserve this? I hate you!" she cries out in disbelief.

"We did what we do? I did what we do to all the boys we find this way. We restore them, V. We wipe their memories clean, and we reconstruct them. We are setting him up perfectly. His life is about to improve massively. New friends, new family, new memories. He'll be the young CEO of an up-and-coming company we've been incubating, and it'll be fine. He'll run that effortlessly, glamorously even."

"I'm never speaking to you again. This is it. If Mom were here, she would be disgusted by you."

"Oh, so what, you're in love with this blackbird? I'm giving him his fucking dream life. You know you can't be with him anyway. We are so close to having this all under our control. You're not going to be the one to let this all slip away."

Vendhaya jumps out of the room, watching Julius's chamber descend, floating beside the chapel in the sky.

16

Lionel sprints down Sixth Avenue with his briefcase, struggling to open the packaging of the new phone he has just purchased. He sees a familiar hotel and quickly enters, glancing in the mirror to fix his sweaty hair and shirt. Approaching the register, Lionel asks for a room while texting and repeatedly calling Sam. He can't reach him. His messages don't deliver, and the calls go straight to voicemail. He enters his room, realizing he forgot to ask for a suite, failing to remember the last time he was in a room this small. Taking off his suit and shirt, he hangs them in the shower to steam. He is still going to attend this dance tonight with Vendhaya. There is nothing else to do, no one else to see.

He takes a shower, puts on his clothes, and prepares to leave. He opens the briefcase, and there are only two bottles. Lionel takes them and places them in his pocket, leaving the briefcase behind as he leaves the room. The sun is now set, and it's an unusually frigid autumn night for the city. A layer of glowing fog glooms below the skyline. Lionel makes his way toward Lincoln Square, where the ballet will be performed. Still stunned by what is happening, he tries to slow his breath. His neck and forehead are throbbingly hot. He has no choice but to ignore his new profound sense of vulnerability.

Approaching the top of the theater's megalithic stairs, Lionel sees a distinctive shadow against the pearl glow of the lobby, drawing his eye to Vendhaya, who is immersed in admiring a painting on the wall. Her mesmerizing golden hair rests on her glitzy, midnight-blue gown. I sneak up behind her. "How come this is the only place I can take you to where you're supposed to dress like that?"

Looking back at him with the smallest smile, she says, "I don't know, but I'd wear this to a picnic with you, Lionel."

"Yeah, sure. Maybe on Lake Como, not at my parents' Irish bog. But I wouldn't take you there anyway. Come on, let's get a drink before the show starts."

Vendhaya slips her hand into Lionel's, her touch a grounding counterpoint to the frenetic energy still swirling within him. The lobby thrums with preperformance excitement, the air thick with anticipation and the perfume of a hundred bouquets. Chandeliers cast glittering prisms of light onto the polished marble floor. But Lionel can't help but steal glances at Vendhaya, etching every detail of her beauty to his memory. The small details in the delicate arch of her neck and the subtle rise and fall of her breath. She radiates an undeniable vitality.

Vendhaya realizes something is off. Why is he so tense? He isn't being himself. He hasn't taken the lusis. Did he not take enough? Did it just not work? Fuck. I left him that briefcase at Cortes Bank, thinking that taking it would trigger a recall.

Holding back her tears, she tries to think up a plan as they go up the stairwell and are escorted to their box.

I need to get him the full dose, she thinks to herself.

The lights dim, the crowds murmur, and whispers go quiet. The show earnestly begins. Sitting on Lionel's right side with her purse on her lap, she fidgets with a bottle of lusis she brought, looking for a moment to dump it in Lionel's drink. But he keeps it held in his left hand. The strings and horns begin to play as the dancers go on stage. Lionel reached for V's hand, his thumb tracing gentle circles into her palm. She squeezes back as their silent conversation weaves through the music.

Then, a group of three men materialize outside their booth. Each bear the stoic imprint of Yakuza loyalty—dark suits stark against intricate tattoos that snake up their arms and necks. The tallest man taps his gun on her shoulder. His face, covered with sunglasses and geometric white ink, says to Vendhaya, "Excuse me," his voice surprisingly soft, laced with a heavy accent. "May I borrow this gentleman for a moment?" He snatches the bag from her lap and hands it to his confidant. Lionel stands up with one eyebrow distinctly raised, obeying their instructions as Vendhaya is quietly forced to stay back with one of the men.

We reach the nearest elevator, where one of the theater patrons lays limp beside it. We enter, and one of the men scans his card, selecting the highest floor. Ascending up the building, the leader notices the man with Vendhaya's purse find something.

"What is it?" he says rapidly, grabbing the purse right out of his partner's hand.

The elevator opens onto the roof of the building.

"I have seen this before. Where have I seen this? This looks so familiar. What is this?" he says, gesturing with the orange-capped bottle in Lionel's face.

"It's just some random shit I like. I must have dropped it, and she must have picked it up for me, not knowing what it was." He nervously feels his jacket pocket for the other two.

"Search him. I swear I have seen this before. Why can't I remember?"

The other men force Lionel onto his knees, removing his belt and jacket. They search his pockets, finding the two other bottles.

"What an unusual surprise."

"What do you mean surprise? Isn't this why we are here right now? Is this not what you're looking for?"

"What? No. I am here because your bullshit company shut down several of our biggest revenue streams. Hanlon exposed partnerships we held with our government for over one hundred years. But because your company came in and started sniffing around, we were shut down. That is why I am here." He shows Lionel a picture of Sam bloodied and pretzeled in the back of a trunk. "Now, the same is going to happen to you. Especially if you don't tell me what this is."

"Whoa, whoa. I don't know what this is. I don't even know how to get more of it. I can tell you what it does to you."

"Tell me what it does to you?" he says, laughing to himself. "Let's just have you take some right now." He gestures to the men.

One of them grabs Lionel, holding him upright as another one of the men unscrews a cap, forcing the bottle into his mouth—forcing him to take the full amount.

Coughing violently, Lionel erupts, "What the fuck was that?"

"So, what happens now?"

"I don't know, I've never taken that much. But I know one thing for sure: whoever makes this stuff killed my driver and threatened me earlier today. They don't want anyone having this shit."

My brain begins to fog, and my body begins to nauseate. I lay flat on my back, staring at the faint, pale stars and the men looking curiously down at me. I close my eyes, and my body escalates into a tingling numbness. My vision, once completely black, flashes to white. I begin to float upward above the building. Looking down,

I see my limp body. The men begin to push it around. They start to argue. The leader pushes the others out of the way and drags me by my arms to the edge of the building, kicking me off the side with no hesitation as Vendhaya rushes out of the door onto the roof. I descend with my body, not knowing what to do. I look across at the buildings, and for a second, I see a reflection.

www.ingramcontent.com/pod-product-compliance
Lightning Source LLC
LaVergne TN
LVHW092055060526
838201LV00047B/1408